A Way with Widows

Other Walker and Company titles by Harold Adams

The Man Who Was Taller Than God
A Perfectly Proper Murder

A Way with Widows

A Carl Wilcox Mystery

Harold Adams

Walker and Company
New York

First published in the United States of America in 1994
by Walker Publishing Company, Inc.

Published simultaneously in Canada by Thomas Allen & Son
Canada, Limited, Markham, Ontario

Library of Congress Cataloging-in-Publication Data
Adams, Harold.
A way with widows: / Harold Adams, 1923–
          p.   cm.
        ISBN 0-8027-3190-2
   1. Wilcox, Carl (Fictitious character)—Fiction.
2. Private investigators—North Dakota—Fiction. I. Title.
         PS3551.D367W37   1994
         813'.54—dc20   94-1245
                             CIP

Printed in the United States of America
2 4 6 8 10 9 7 5 3 1

*This book is for my uncle Sidney Dickey,
genesis of Carl Wilcox, cowboy, hobo,
soldier, convict, and practical joker supreme,
who loved the poetry of Omar Khayyám,
all merry widows, and one pet black snake,
which he named after his only wife.*

Acknowledgments

This forgetful author would like to acknowledge the invaluable aid from friends who live or have lived in the town where I spent my childhood summers. Their memories, more retentive than mine, have provided details re time and place in South Dakota that have made it possible to write authentic background for Carl Wilcox and his world.

First there is Gail Myers, who always knew more and remembered it better than I could. Then there is H. T. Desnoyers, a lifetime resident of Corden, fascinated by the early years and more than willing to dig up and pass on details and atmosphere.

I would also like to acknowledge the editorial savvy and support of Michael Seidman, who has been involved with Carl's saga, off and on, for fourteen years. He has always kept the faith. Lord knows, I needed it.

Finally, I thank Barbara Mayor, who remains my favorite critic and volunteer editor.

A Way with Widows

1

It WAS NEAR midday, on a Tuesday in June, when I pulled up in front of Annabelle's house in Red Ford, North Dakota. Wind off the prairie tousled my nephew Kip's hair as he scrambled off the duplex steps and ran toward my Model T. He was standing on the berm by the time I turned off the motor and climbed down to greet him. He remembered he was thirteen now, and too old to jump on me, but didn't think to stick out his small hand until I offered mine. As we solemnly shook hands he asked if I was going to find out who'd stabbed Mr. Feist to death in the widow's house next door.

"Since your ma has given me the job, you know blamed well I've no choice but to give it a whirl," I said.

He nodded with perfect understanding, and told me his mother was real excited and had already made doughnuts for me and right now was doing a devil's food cake with fudge frosting.

"That ought to make you glad I came."

He nodded happily.

We went up the front walk and took the outside steps to the second floor, where Annabelle grabbed me at the kitchen door and hung on for about two seconds before letting go and hauling down the old marshmallow tin she stored her doughnuts in. Next came fresh coffee and questions about Ma and Pa and her son Hank who was finishing his junior year at Corden High while helping run the hotel weekends and evenings.

By the time that was covered I was eating my third doughnut and she felt it was appropriate to get down to the subject at hand.

"As you might imagine," she told me, "poor Stella's about out of her mind over this awful thing and I just can't think of much else myself. You don't know her, of course, but you won't have to any more than see her to know perfectly well she couldn't possibly've done what they're accusing her of. And once you get to know her you'll see why you've just got to help her."

Annabelle had never believed any friend she accepted had a fault or failing. If you pointed out that a friend maybe talked a little too much she'd say, "Well, that's just the way she is and she can't help that now, can she?"

Since Annabelle considered any critic of her friends beneath contempt, I avoided putting them down no matter how hopeless they were.

So I swilled coffee and ate doughnuts while Kip sat by, awed by his mother's generosity to me. He'd never seen anybody get more than one doughnut at one sitting before in his whole life and made the mistake of commenting on that. Annabelle promptly decided what we were about to discuss wasn't for his innocent ears.

"You can go to your room now," she told him. "Your uncle and I have things to talk about that couldn't possibly interest you."

"That's okay," he assured her, "I won't get bored."

"Go," she said. He sighed and went.

She had already told me most of the story over the telephone when she made her panic call the day before, and the details she offered didn't add up to anything that made me feel any confidence about my chances of saving her friend.

After Annabelle was satisfied that she'd fortified me against any doubts about Stella's loyalty, fidelity, and absolute purity, she handed me the local daily paper, which laid out the bloody details of the affair.

The body of Aaron H. Feist had been found in a puddle of gore halfway up the stairs at the neighbors' shortly after dark on Sunday night. The renter of the house, Darlene Singer, and her daughter, Carrie, had told the police they did not realize anyone else was in the house until they heard what sounded like someone falling on the stairs. When they came out they found Mr. Feist bleeding on the landing.

The police report said he had been stabbed over a dozen times with a long knife. They couldn't find the weapon in the house, but a search of the yard turned up a butcher knife beside the back step with bloodstains between the handle and the blade.

Stella admitted it came from her kitchen.

"So what," I asked, "besides the fact it was Stella's knife, makes the cops think she ventilated her hubby?"

"Somebody stole it," Annabelle told me angrily. "Stella's never used that awful thing—it always terrified her. She uses a paring knife or ham slicer for anything she cuts in the kitchen."

I didn't figure she'd ever had anything big as Aaron to carve before, but kept that to myself and asked how the couple got along.

For the first time she looked embarrassed.

"Well, that's a problem," she confessed. "They hadn't been close for a long time. Aaron was really just an impossible man. I mean, he had this silly dance band and was always off somewhere playing in dumb little towns, so he was gone just about all of the time and never did anything around his own house but always found time to help his neighbors—"

"You mean Stella figured he was getting more than home cooking?"

"Well, for heaven's sake, who wouldn't? I mean, why would a true husband always be gone out of his own house, neglecting his wife?"

"What about the neighbor's daughter—what was going on there?"

"Carrie? You can just forget about her. She's an innocent, simpleminded girl who isn't interested in men, and besides, her mother watches her like a hawk. No, take my word for it, there was absolutely nothing going on there."

"So why was he killed in their house?"

"That's what you'll have to find out."

"I'll need a little help. All I've heard so far are reasons why your friend didn't trust or like her husband. How about names of other people that might have wanted to do the carving job?"

"Stella didn't hate him! Don't think like that. I'm certain if you just check around a little, you'll find plenty of people who were mad at him. You'll have to talk to folks, the way you always do—nobody's better at drawing them out. His friends in the band, maybe people at the store . . . ?"

"Uh-huh. How simple's this Carrie?"

"Well, she can read and even do some figures, but she couldn't keep up in school and had to give up. She helps her mother around the house. Carrie is a sweet but painfully shy child."

"Good looking?"

"Well, yes, she is. Very pretty, in fact. Too doll-like for men, I'm sure."

"How old's the mother?"

"Oh, probably near fifty."

"Good looking?"

"I'm sure you'd think so. But don't get ideas about her and Aaron. He wouldn't be chasing after her."

"So how come he was always helping this pair? What'd he do over there?"

"Well, things like repairing wallpaper that started to peel in the dining room, taking clinkers out of their furnace, and hauling ashes from the basement—things women can't do."

"All as a good neighbor?"

"Of course. He was good-hearted, but shiftless. If he'd had any proper sense he would've worked in his father's store and been manager and finally owner, and he'd have amounted to something and they would've had lots of money, but he was too crazy about playing with the ridiculous band and having people fuss over that."

"Did Stella think Aaron was after Carrie?"

"I don't think she really believed he was trying to, you know, seduce her. But he had told Stella how nice it was to talk to a pretty girl who didn't let him know he was stupid and lazy."

"Stella did, I suppose."

"Well, he was!"

"And if she told him often enough he might get over it, huh?"

"Oh, Carl, you'd take the man's side, wouldn't you?"

"Not me. I like women's sides. All of them."

She got her wise look, figuring she could depend on my weakness. "You'll like Stella. She's very attractive and high-spirited."

"And smart?"

"That's no fault."

"Not always. It seems to me I remember Hank mentioning this neighbor lady. He was pretty impressed."

"Oh, yes," said Annabelle a little too casually, "he's very fond of her."

"What'd she think of him?"

"Why ask that? She's nearly old enough to be his mother, for heaven's sake."

"He sure didn't talk like he thought of her that way."

"Well, you know Hank, he's at the stage where he's a little gaga over any woman who's pretty at all and gives him a second glance."

"That didn't have anything to do with your letting him finish high school in Corden, did it?"

"I let him go because his grandparents needed him and they couldn't depend on you."

She had me there and I didn't figure it'd do much good telling her how tough it had been to convince her son he couldn't come with me to rescue the damsel in distress.

When he'd seen me off he'd insisted I keep him posted on developments.

I called Stella's lawyer and a frosty lady answered, demanded I state my business, and with obvious reluctance, called her boss to the phone. His name was Al Hamilton and his voice crackled. Yes, Stella had told him about me and he could see me the next morning at eleven. He could spare about fifteen minutes.

It didn't sound too promising.

Stella was being held by the police pending bail. I decided to visit City Hall and see if they'd let me talk to the prisoner, but of course they wouldn't. The only reason the desk sergeant talked to me at all was he suspected I was a guy who'd been romancing the suspect. He pretended sympathy at first, saying she was a lady in real trouble, which would make any man naturally want to help, and of course the fact she wasn't exactly ugly was some on her side.

I told him I'd never seen her.

He was offended. "If you've never met her, why the hell you want to see her now?"

I explained about my sister's relationship and that she'd called on me because I'd done some police work in South Dakota.

"I know nobody here's panting for my help, but I got to go through the motions for Sis."

"You been a cop?" The notion brought a grin. "You look more like a bum."

"I've been both. They're not as far apart as you might think."

The grin went and he said okay, you've gone through the motions, now go through the door there behind you.

I didn't have any trouble finding it.

$\triangledown$

2

It was always a wonder to Ma and Pa that Annabelle and her husband, Scott, thought they had a perfect match even though he was a traveling salesman on the road every weekday. It made good sense to me. That way they had a honeymoon every weekend and never got sick of each other. Neither of the boys felt there was anything unusual about their lives, and I suspected Kip wouldn't mind if his father only showed up for Christmas and the Fourth of July. When Scott came home he always set his suitcase down by the door and headed for Annabelle. Kip immediately opened the suitcase and dug out *The Saturday Evening Post, Collier's,* and *Liberty* and went through them. He liked the cartoons in the first two, and by the time he was eleven he was reading the short stories in *Liberty.* Scott wasn't sure he should approve of that but finally decided it was harmless. He couldn't remember reading anything in his life that changed him for good or bad.

Since this was Tuesday night, the man of the house was gone and I ate ham loaf and scalloped potatoes with Annabelle, and Kip talked about his teacher, who lost her temper and gave a kid in class a fat lip when he sassed. It was clear Kip enjoyed the action, and it made me realize one of the reasons most classmates liked me was that I brought so much excitement into our one-room school. Somehow I was always getting belted or paddled.

After the meal I eased outside and wandered around the neighborhood. The Feist home was dark and silent, but the

one beyond, where the Singers lived, showed light in the
kitchen and a bedroom upstairs. From the narrow, fairly
sharp-slanted roof, I guessed there were only two bedrooms.
I went down the alley and considered the backyard, which
had a crabapple tree and a garage that looked unused. It
seemed wise to wait until daylight to try visiting the woman
and her daughter. I am not the kind of man many people will
be pleased to find on their doorstep at night.

I cranked up my Model T, drove the quiet streets into
downtown, which was peaceful as church on Saturday night,
and crossed the triple truss bridge over the Red River to the
Eastside.

The Eastside in those days claimed more neon tubing per
square block than any city but New York and more bars per
capita than anyplace else in the world. It got popular and
successful during Prohibition when speakeasies were its
primary business. After repeal they brought in gambling to
keep the outlaw tradition. It probably went on before '33 but
it wasn't that important in the beginning. There was no
entertainment. Customers found all they wanted in glasses,
slot machines, gaming tables, and each other. They didn't
need jokers, singers, or musicians to know they were having
a good time.

I went into Jacob's place, which wasn't one of the newer,
classy joints. It had old wood and dark walls, a heavy bar,
and a moderate crowd. There were two rows of slot machines
getting steady work mostly from stocky women, and about
half the stools at the long bar were unoccupied. There were
even a couple women perched near the front. I found space
not far from the men's room in back and asked for a beer.
The hefty barman handed it over and took my money
without a glance at me, and I said, "Hi, Willie, how's Myrt?"

He squinted and grinned, showing his tooth gap.

"For Christ's sake, its Wilcox, the snakeman. You still
wearing Pearl under your shirt?"

"Don't remind me of the tragedy."

"Somebody shot her?"

"She froze in her box on the back porch when we had a sudden freeze. All six feet of her."

"You're probably lucky. One of these days she'd have swallowed you sure. What the hell're you doing in town?"

"You heard of the Feist stabbing?"

"You think I'm deaf and blind? Hell yes. His wife did it, I hear."

"My sister thinks she didn't. Called me for help."

"She'd get more help from the snake. What the hell're you gonna do?"

"Look around. You know this Feist guy?"

"Oh sure, he was a regular. We talked lotsa times. Good kinda guy."

"Ever come around with his wife?"

"Stella? Yeah, she was here a couple times. A real piece, you know?"

"How'd they get along?"

He laughed. "Funny you should ask. The last time I seen her, she belted Aaron and walked out alone. I hafta admit, I get a lot bigger kick out of it when the wife socks the guy."

"Ever hear why she hit him?"

"Man, I don't ask."

"Any of the guys from his band come around?"

"Frenchy does, yeah. The old tenor sax man. He'll probably be their leader now."

"He's old?"

"Nah, that's just what I call him. He's not thirty yet but he's got old eyes, you know? Like Hoagy Carmichael. He's a comer. He'll dump Gus, their drummer, and get somebody hot."

"How come Aaron kept an old drummer?"

"Oh, he'd known Gus forever—Gus got him his first dance job. That's the way Aaron was, loyal as hell. He'd have kept Gus till he dropped."

"But he couldn't get along with his wife?"

"All I know about are a couple nights. One they got on, the other she slugged him. Maybe they both liked it that way.

Some do, you know? You ever see what happens when a stranger steps in to protect a woman from her man? The woman tries to kill him. How can you figure 'em?"

"He ever talk about his wife when he was here alone?"

"Never," he said, straightening up. "Not once. Aaron was a gentleman."

When he moved off to take booth orders from a waitress, I went over and donated five nickels to a slot machine while rubbernecking around. Only two faces looked familiar, but they were just guys I'd seen around and I didn't know their names.

I drifted east hitting bars that occupied every other building in the block, talking to bartenders when I could and to customers if they were willing. Everybody'd heard about the murder; most assumed the wife did it but none really knew anything.

In Blacky's, a small joint near an intersection, I met Lars, who claimed he knew a cop who'd checked out a complaint at the Feists' a year before. He said the loving couple had been fighting in their backyard and the neighbor kid got in it and flattened the husband. He told me the cop's name was Maltby. There was no problem about the address; it was next door to his own.

Back at Annabelle's I found she'd left a light on and made up a bed for me on the couch. I used the toilet, peeled down, crawled into the sack, and thought about the coming day for a good ten seconds before corking off.

▽

3

THE LAST TIME I'd slept in Annabelle's place, Kip, who was then eight years old, had been sitting on the floor beside the couch watching when I opened my eyes. He told me my chin was all black and wanted to know if I'd been drunk the night before. It seems he'd heard his father discussing me with his mother. When I rolled a cigarette he informed he his dad didn't have to do that, he bought them ready-made.

"Some guys can't do much of anything for themselves," I said.

"Can you teach me how to fight?" he asked.

"Ask your brother."

"I don't think that'd work. I wanna know how to fight him."

That was a tall ambition considering Hank was five years older and a natural scrapper to boot, so I told Kip his best approach was to make friends. But I always remembered the little guy's crust.

This morning I heard him sneeze in his room down the hall, and while I was remembering five years back he beat me to the bathroom.

By the time I got to the kitchen Annabelle had bacon fried, coffee made, and eggs and pancakes under way. She was always generous with breakfast, but I suspected this splurge on a weekday was part of her program to keep me happy on this visit and willing to rescue her pal Stella.

I started telling her about my evening's work, and she right away sighed and said she hoped I wouldn't start hanging around bars this trip. It didn't help any when I told her about the bartender's comments. She wouldn't believe Stella would clobber Aaron out in public like that.

So I told her I tried to visit her friend at the jail and was sent off but had an appointment with the attorney and we'd see where that took us. That cheered her up some, and she told me she knew she could depend on me.

When I got past the dragon in lawyer Hamilton's outer office, he squinted at me and said in his crackling voice, "You're not very tall."

"You're not very young," I answered.

His tight mouth opened a slit he might have considered a smile while he peered at me over half-glasses underlining pale blue eyes. He had a smooth dome, sunken cheeks, a frame of white fuzz coddling his ears, and more jaw than he needed.

"Your sister, Annabelle, tells me you want to help," he said.

"I promised her I'd see."

"You don't look like a cop."

"You think Annabelle'd lie?"

"She might if she thought it'd help her friend. Your sister carries loyalty to unrealistic lengths."

"It's not a bad flaw."

He sighed and nodded. "I'll admit," he said, "I'm inordinately fond of her, but this isn't a promising case. If you're determined to get involved, I may as well lay out the facts as I know them. And let's get one thing straight. If you're going to be any use at all, forget anything Annabelle's told you. She's objective as a doting mother. But I suppose you already know that?"

I nodded.

"Very well. The bare bones: Saturday night, about ten-thirty, Aaron Feist was stabbed to death on the stairway of his neighbors' house. Mrs. Singer, the owner, lives there with her simpleminded daughter, and it's common knowledge that Aaron was very friendly with them, visiting often and doing various chores to help them out. On the evening in question, Mrs. Singer claims she didn't know Aaron was in the house. That she and her daughter were in her bedroom together with the door closed and suddenly heard frightening noises on the stairway. They were too terrified to look until long after everything was still, and when Mrs. Singer finally came out to investigate she found Aaron dead on the landing. She managed to walk around him downstairs to the telephone and called the police."

"Do the mother and daughter sleep in the same room?"

"I don't know."

"You think Aaron was messing with the daughter?"

"Mrs. Singer denies it. Vehemently. Stella's certain of it but has no real evidence, and I've warned her not to broadcast her opinion but I'm afraid it's already widespread."

"How simple you think the daughter is?"

"It's hard to say. She's unnaturally shy. I'm told she has a marvelous memory of anything she's read, seen, or heard. She's not the sort to do much reading so she's not cluttered up with that, but she can read and write. Oh, whenever anybody asks her what happened that night, she says ask Mama."

"What's the business about the knife?"

"It belonged to the Feists, all right. Stella admits it. But claims she never used it for anything and that it'd been missing for a week or so."

"If she never used it, how come she missed it?"

"I asked the same question—so did the police. She says it was a big thing and you didn't have to use it to notice it and she thought Aaron borrowed it and hadn't mentioned it because it didn't seem important."

"And they found it in the drawer?"

"No, it was beside the back stoop, on the ground."

"All wiped off?"

"Yes. In a way that might help us some. If she'd really used it and had the presence of mind to wipe it clean, it hardly seems natural she'd drop it on the way back into her house after she'd stabbed him."

"I don't figure Aaron made a living running a band. What else'd he do?"

"He inherited a share of the Feist Haberdashery from his father and went through the motions of working there now and then, but it's actually run by Gene Fox, who was the old man's general manager and owns half the place."

"How's Fox feel about his half-assed partner?"

"As far as anybody knows, fine. He's a very steady type."

"And with Aaron gone, Stella gets his half interest in the store?"

"She's the only beneficiary. They had no children and Aaron was an only child."

"Is there anything in Stella's favor?"

"Not much. She's a mite flashy for this town and has a notorious temper. Worst of all, most folks think she's too smart for her own good. She's positive there was hanky-panky with the neighbor's daughter. Now normally I'd be happy to defend about any woman against a murder, especially if she had kids, because men just don't like to convict women for murder. But this woman'll get their backs up and the man was unmercifully slashed. It was a mess and they got pictures of it nobody can forget."

"Any word around about Stella doing some freelancing while her hubby was off blowing his horn nights?"

He leaned back and dropped his hands in his lap.

"I guess that's something you should check up on. She tells me no. I haven't heard anything, but I don't circulate among people who'd pass on such gossip. If there is anything, the defense would certainly like to know in advance."

"Yeah. I've got a line—I'll let you know what's on the end of it."

The telephone rang; his dragon answered and called to say it was for him and I left.

4

DURING LUNCH WITH Annabelle I asked what she knew of the guys in Aaron's band.

"Not much. You probably ought to talk with Gus. He's the drummer and works days as a barber. Cuts Hank's and Scott's hair."

I found out where his shop was and drifted around.

He wasn't there. His partner, a lanky ancient with baggy eyes and loose store teeth, said the man was in mourning.

"Ain't been here since Aaron's wife done him in. Ol' Gus, he thought the world of Aaron."

He gave me Gus's home address. A stocky woman with light brown hair answered my knock and greeted me with a measuring look that found me wanting. I asked if Gus was around.

"Why?" she asked in a voice sweet as a drill sergeant's.

"It's personal," I said.

"He's indisposed," she told me.

Her blue housedress fit a little soon, so the buttons puckered the cloth across the top. She brought her arms up and folded them firmly across her chest.

"You his granddaughter?" I asked.

That made her grin and tilt her head, producing dimples and a come-on look that worked.

"No," she said as her voice softened, "I'm his landlady but that's a cute line. You don't look like a snake oil salesman, what're you after?"

"A little talk with Gus. It won't cost him a dime."

"He's all shook up over a friend being murdered, so he's resting. I don't want him bothered."

"What makes you think somebody'd want to bother him?"

"You're Annabelle's brother, the one she brought up from South Dakota, right?"

I confessed I was.

"And Annabelle doesn't believe Stella killed Aaron, and you're going to dig up all the dirt, huh?"

"You read palms, too?" I asked.

"I know about you."

"Then you know I'm not here to accuse Gus of killing his bandleader. How about you tell him I want to talk with him?"

"Let him in," said a voice from behind her.

She unfolded her arms, pushed the screen open, and stood aside as I passed, catching the faint scent of shampoo and fresh coffee.

We sat in a small, shadowed living room. The blinds were drawn against the summer sun, and Gus looked frail, white, and gloomy. His landlady sat to his right.

I said I was sorry about his friend.

He nodded.

"I'd like to find out some things about Aaron," I said. "You mind talking about him and the band a little?"

"Yeah, I mind. The hell with it."

"Okay. You don't care who killed him, is that it?"

He flushed angrily. "What kinda thing's that to say?"

"What else should I think if you won't help?"

"Who the hell are you? What're you gonna do about anything?"

His landlady horned in and told him I was Annabelle's brother, the fellow who caught some killers in South Dakota.

"Annabelle wants him to prove Stella didn't do it to Aaron."

Gus stared at me. "You figure you can do that?" he asked.

"I can try."

"They say it was done with her knife and it was right next

door and Stella was already mad because Aaron'd been hanging around that simple girl. . . ."

"Yeah, it looks plain enough. But I'd like to know if anybody else might've come out ahead with Aaron gone."

"Stella'd do best. She'd inherit half the store, which is what she married him for in the first place. Now she can find a guy who amounts to something."

He said "amounts to something" with contempt.

"What about Frenchy?" I asked.

His eyes brightened just a tad. "Well, sure, Frenchy'll be taking over the band. He's wanted to all along."

"Didn't he like you?"

"He had his way, I'd been dumped the first week he came on. He thinks it's a crime to get old."

"How'd he get on with Aaron?"

"Well, you couldn't hardly fight with him unless you were Stella, but he ragged him a lot. He wanted him to dump me and Ted."

"What's Ted play?"

"Piano. He plays fine. Can't do much but chords but he does 'em good, and he's great about setting up the stands and the music when we start a job anyplace and never goofs off."

"Who goofs off?"

"Well, Doug comes back from intermissions late. That's about the only thing ever made Aaron mad, but even then he didn't yell or get nasty. Aaron was a sweet man. . . ." His voice failed him and he blinked and stared at the bare floor a moment.

"Any other problems with the band? Complaints about payoffs?"

"Oh, Frenchy bitched lots of times when we had a percentage deal. He'd claim the crowd was bigger than we got paid for. He was cute, though. He always said he trusted Aaron—it was the dance hall owners he figured were cheating us and Aaron was too soft to fight over it."

"You think he was?"

"Maybe." The confession cost him a little and he thought about it and finally sighed.

"You trying to figure Frenchy might've done Aaron? That won't get you anyplace. He's a turd but he wouldn't kill anybody."

"What kind of a job's he got?"

"Drives a dump truck for the county. It works out pretty good because he's off at four o'clock every day. Of course, he don't get much sleep when we do a Tuesday job. But that don't seem to bother him none."

"You think the band'll go on?" I asked.

"Not for me."

"You feel bad about that, huh?"

"I feel bad about Aaron. The band's no big deal for me. I liked the extra money, but the nights've been getting longer lately and riding back and forth's a pain in the ass. I won't miss it."

I didn't believe him but kept that to myself.

"What's this Doug play?"

"Trumpet and trombone. His trombone's a valve job—he don't know about sliding."

"He unhappy about the payoffs?"

"Well, he goes along with Frenchy. He wants more money and he don't care what way."

"And the piano player, Ted?"

"Ted's no trouble anytime with anybody. He just does his job and laughs a lot."

"Isn't there another rhythm man?"

"Uh-huh. Ed West. He plays a sousaphone. He don't hardly talk at all."

"How old's the band?"

"Oh God, going on six, seven years. All but Max. We had a guy before him whose wife made him quit. Couldn't put up with him gone so many nights, but the real trouble was she figured he was messing around. It didn't hurt any. Max is good already and he'll be better. He's only in high school. He mows lawns and does odd jobs."

▽

5

THERE WAS ONE Maltby listed in the telephone directory and my call was answered by a chirpy woman who said yeah, her husband was the cop. And sure, he'd be around if I wanted to drop by—he worked the night shift.

Officer Maltby was under a lilac bush in the front yard, clipping off dead blossoms, when I arrived. He greeted me as friendly as if he welcomed bums every day, so I laid out why I was there without hardly any lies, and it didn't surprise me when he grinned about how the desk sergeant had handled me.

"Old Colvin's a hardass," he said. "You couldn't expect anything better from him. Let's go sit on the porch. I got to be on my feet all night."

Before getting around to Hank he told me the house was his wife's, left to her by her widowed mother, who'd gone off to live in California with a sister. It was a small white bungalow in pretty good condition and he let me know he wasn't too proud to appreciate it even if it had been a gift from his mother-in-law.

Eventually he got around to the fight I was asking about, which happened a year before.

"I was on days then and got this call late in the afternoon. A woman said there was a domestic scrap at the Feists'. So I went over and found the husband, Aaron, sitting on the back stoop looking pained, and his wife was out of sight. Hank, the neighbor kid, was standing around with a sheepish look on his mug. When I asked what was going on, they both said nothing.

For a moment he was silent and then he gave me a
sly look. "You know Max is a buddy of your nephew Ha

"No."

"Hank's one that hated Aaron. If he wasn't off south,
the guy they'd've picked up."

"Why?"

"He's in love with Stella, that's why. And last year he lai
Aaron out. Maybe you'd oughtta talk to your nephew. See
how Annabelle likes that notion."

"A couple neighbors moved in then and this one woman tells me the Feists were fighting in the yard and Hank came running from next door and knocked Aaron down.

"So I got Aaron and your nephew in the house, and Mrs. Feist came down from upstairs and after a while she told me that she and her husband had a spat and he'd made her mad enough she started pounding him and he'd run out the back, stumbled on the steps, and she'd jumped on him and made him mad enough to hit her one when he got up, and then your nephew showed up and smacked him with a flying tackle that about broke his back. The upshot was, nobody wanted to make any charges, so I warned them against disturbing the peace again and went back to my beat."

"You ever find out what started the spat?"

"Nope. I knew they'd scrapped before and it was mostly because she didn't like him off on dance jobs meeting other women and all that."

"Did the neighbors think he was getting any from the neighbor's daughter?"

"Sure. These are nice people but they need a little spice in life and the best of 'em can't believe Aaron's so pure he helps his neighbor out just because she's his neighbor." He watched me for a moment and smiled a little sadly. "They kinda think, too, that Hank didn't come running to save the lady just because he's a natural-born hero for ladies in distress. Not even his ma thought that."

"She thought it," I said, "but she knew what the neighbors'd figure."

"You're probably right."

Officer Maltby was a kind cop.

"You think Aaron was maybe a woman chaser in general?" I asked.

He crossed his legs and clasped his hands over his raised knee. "Well now, I've thought about that some. I wonder about why he's working with this half-assed band that's not going anywhere and not making any real money. And I've talked with some people, like the new boy Max, and he says

there are girls from Red Ford who'll drive up to sixty miles
just to go where this crummy band's at. Now let's face it,
that's a kind of thing that has to make a man feel pretty
important and wanted and when that's a big deal for him,
it's not likely he's gonna look the other way when some cutie
gives him the old come-hither eye. As a matter of fact, it's
enough to make even me wish I'd taken up drums or a horn."

"But if that's what he goes for, how come he'd get involved
with a simpleminded girl right next door?"

"Maybe he thinks he's being a nice guy. Maybe he's feeling
guilty about the road fluff."

"So why'd he make things tougher for his wife, who's
bound to see something screwy's going on?"

Officer Maltby's eyes half closed.

"I've thought about that, too. I figure a woman like Stella
gives him so much trouble he just naturally doesn't ever feel
guilty about cheating on her. In fact, more than likely he
wants her to know he is. Guys can be damned weird, you
know?"

He knew where Max lived and told me the way there. I
heard the alto sax from a couple houses away. He was playing
something sweet and easy I'd never heard before and I stood
on the porch a few seconds until he finished it before
knocking.

He was a tall, rangy kid with square shoulders, thin dark
hair that'd never reach middle age, and a wide, chiseled
mouth. He looked at me through the screen when I introduced myself as Hank's uncle and grinned as if he remembered something goofy I'd done and Hank had told about.

He invited me in. It was a simple house with spare
furniture and everything in place like a cleaning lady'd just
been through. There was the familiar picture of the lone wolf
on one wall and Inspiration Falls on another. He sat down
on the couch beside his gleaming saxophone and I parked
in the corner chair facing him.

I asked him how the future looked for a sax man and he
said it might be okay.

"Frenchy's gonna keep the band going?"

Max nodded. "We talked this morning. I'm gonna be lead alto." He grinned. "That's because Saturday I'll be the only alto. He's got a drummer from the Eastside and the next week a guy from Oakley'll join up. Frenchy's already got an okay from the dance hall owner in Corden to come shy one member this Saturday."

"Frenchy doesn't waste much time, does he?"

"He's been thinking about this a long time," said Max and then looked embarrassed. "I don't mean about Aaron dying, I mean about starting a new band. He liked Aaron, but he thought he was an awful bandleader. We never practiced except on the job and Aaron couldn't even read music. So he could learn a number perfect after two times— you'd think a guy running a band could read music, for gosh sakes."

"How come Frenchy didn't cut loose long ago?"

"Well, Aaron was in real good with dance hall people, and it's not easy to find guys who can play and have jobs that can get away to work two or three nights a week. None of us with Aaron would feel right about leaving him except maybe Doug, and even he wasn't sure."

He talked some more about the band before I worked him around to how Aaron dealt with the willing women on the circuit.

Max shook his head.

"I don't care what Stella or anybody else says, Aaron didn't fool around on the road. He was scared, that's a fact. Women made him nervous. Oh, you could tell he wanted them to like him and he'd talk nice and friendly when they'd hang around, but he never took one out to the car or even for a walk or something to drink. The only ones he paid attention to were wallflower types. Ones too shy to push him. He'd smile at them from the stand. And ones that'd sit real close he'd kid with a little or even tell them he was dedicating a number to them if they were real regulars—and a lot of 'em were. Aaron was a really nice guy. Really."

"Were you surprised Hank lit into him?"

I could feel him withdraw.

"I don't know about that," he said. "I haven't talked with Hank since that happened."

"You think he had a case on Stella?"

"Hank has a very special feeling about just about all women. He liked Aaron, too, but if he saw him or Christ himself raise a hand to a woman he'd go nuts."

"Even when the woman had been pounding hell out of the guy?"

"Well, maybe he didn't see that part. Maybe he came out just when Aaron had finally lost his temper and belted her."

"Did Hank ever ask you if Aaron messed around on the road?"

He took long enough to answer, so I could tell he was trying to decide what that'd give away. Finally he met my eye.

"Yeah, he did. I told him just what I've told you."

"You think he believed you?"

"Hank wouldn't think I'd lie."

"He might think you were wrong, though."

He shrugged, but I could tell that'd been the case and it worried him. It might even have had something to do with the fact they hadn't talked after the backyard brawl a year ago.

"You talk with Hank before he went down to Corden?" I asked.

He shook his head. "I was pretty busy, being new with the band and all."

I was just about to leave when the telephone rang, so I said good-bye and started down the walk. I hadn't gone far when he called to tell me it was my sister, trying to reach me.

I went back and Annabelle said Stella was out on bail and when could I talk with her.

"Where is she?"

"Here with me."

"Okay. Tell her I'd like to talk with her alone at her house. I'll go there right now."

"Why not here?"

"Because I want to talk to her alone. That's the best way."

"Don't get any ideas," she warned.

"I haven't had an idea in months. Send her home. I'll talk to you later."

$\triangledown$

6

I T WAS HARD to believe the dark-eyed, slim-bodied woman at the door could be Stella. She didn't look big enough to reach a man's head with a punch, let alone chase him out of the house and pummel him on the ground. Her light brown hair was bobbed and shiny, her mouth wide, full-lipped, and full of small, even teeth white as a Quaker's collar.

"Hello, Carl," she said in a voice next door to husky. I wondered if it got that way from yelling at her husband, and began to think I was heading for trouble when my mind refused to consider it.

"Hi, Stella."

She pushed the screen open and waved me inside.

I passed her, catching a faint whiff of scented powder, and turned left into a living room off the hall flanked by a stairway to the second floor. The room was medium big for our territory and full of overstuffed furniture with no frills or covers to guard against greasy heads or grimy hands. I guessed no kids had ever occupied it for long and not too many guests. The pictures on the walls had lots of flowers and no people, animals, or mountains.

I sat in a corner chair as she parked on the couch to my right and crossed her trim ankles. Her dark blue dress had no trimming and didn't miss a curve.

"Hank has your eyes," she told me.

"How come I never missed them?"

She laughed a good one and folded her hands in her lap like a little girl in church.

"He told me a few things about you," she said.

"I hope he lied a lot."

The second laugh was even warmer. She seemed ready to have a good time.

"Did he tell you anything about me?" she asked.

"I think he was careful not to."

That brought a quick frown. "What's that mean?"

"He probably was afraid he'd give something away."

"Really? Like what?"

"He was stuck on you."

She made a face. "What an unpleasant expression. It makes me sound like flypaper."

"What'd you and your husband scrap about?"

"We're going to get down to business now, huh? All right. We didn't actually fight that much. The one Hank stopped was the only one where anybody got hurt or I disgraced myself—"

"You slapped him in a bar once."

She blushed and swallowed. "Okay, there were two times, but that didn't amount to anything—"

"What brought that one on?"

There was a flicker of her eyelids before she decided to be honest.

"He accused me of leading Hank on. It made me lose my temper. He did things like that to justify his catting around with the camp followers of the band."

"Guys from the band claim he was afraid of women—wouldn't touch 'em."

"I'm not surprised. They all thought he was a saint. He was way too cute for any of those fools. An honest woman hasn't a chance with a lying, tricky husband."

"Then you're not exactly shook up over his murder?"

She leaned forward, letting me know she trusted me and felt she could tell me the truth. "I won't miss him—to be honest, I'm relieved. But I'm not the kind of idiot who'd murder him with my own butcher knife. I'll tell you just how it is, Carl. That man didn't even arouse hate in me at the end. What I was trying to do was drive him out of my house, because I earned this place—I furnished it, cared for it, and wanted it for mine. It meant nothing to him. Nothing meant anything to him but that damned band and that stupid horn. He could have been somebody in town, carried on the store his father ran that was the best of its kind around here. He wasn't even a real musician. Did you know he couldn't read music?"

"Yeah. Where were you when he was stabbed?"

She drew back, looking hurt. "In my bedroom, upstairs."

"Did you know he was out?"

"No. He had his room. I have mine."

"How long's it been like that?"

"A long time." Her expression was sorrowful.

"You saying you two never slept together?"

"Not in the last eight years."

"Since he started the band?"

"That's right."

"Whose idea was that?"

"What difference does that make?"

"Well, if it was yours, I'd figure there was good reason for him to be looking for something, on the road or next door. And I'd wonder why you'd care who he slept with."

"I wasn't fond of looking the fool," she said impatiently. "And I'm not going to talk any more about this subject."

I let that rest a minute, crossed my legs, and rolled a smoke. She watched my hands. When I lit up she sat back and crossed her legs, keeping the skirt over her knees.

"When'd you find out Aaron had been murdered?" I asked.

"Around eleven. I heard something going on next door, car doors slamming and voices that seemed unnaturally loud for so late. I went into Aaron's room and looked through his window facing the Singer house, which was all lit up. I couldn't imagine what was going on and went to the stairwell and called 'Aaron?' a couple times, thinking he was in the kitchen having a cup of warm milk, which he did sometimes, but of course there was no answer so I slipped on my robe and went down, and finally I went out on the back stoop and an officer came out of the Singers' and over to me and said he was sorry, there'd been a bad accident. It took several seconds for me to realize he was telling me the accident had happened to my husband. Just about when I understood him, another officer in plain clothes came and he asked if I'd been home all evening. I could feel them examining me and realized pretty soon they got a bad impression because I didn't get hysterical or weepy. My lawyer, Al—you met him, didn't you?—he told me they thought I was in shock at first and figured it was because I'd killed Aaron in a blind rage."

"When'd they arrest you?"

"Monday morning. I couldn't believe it. They'd been talking to people. Like Darlene Singer and the guys from the band who said I fought all the time with Aaron. They showed me my old butcher knife and asked if I could identify it. I said yes it was mine and had been missing. They said they found blood in the space between the handle and the blade. I can't believe that. It's honest to God been missing for over a week—maybe a year for all I know since I never used it and just noticed it was gone lately. I figured Aaron used it to cut up cardboard boxes so he could burn them in the trash barrel out back."

"Who do you think killed him?" I asked.

"I can't imagine, but it seems most likely it was Darlene. She's fanatical about Carrie, and what the hell, it happened on her stairway landing, not mine."

"You think she snuck over here, stole your knife, and saved it for the butchering?"

"All I know is, I didn't kill him and she had good reason and the body was in her house. We never locked our doors, so someone could've snuck in easy."

"You slept okay that night?"

"Like a baby. But even if I hadn't, if someone crept in quietly, I'd not have heard them downstairs. This is a fairly

big house, and well made so you don't hear floors creaking
or the hinges squeaking."

I asked her if Aaron had ever discussed the band with her
and she said certainly not, it was the last thing she cared to
hear about.

I stood up to leave and she walked to the door with me,
very lightly putting her hand on my arm as I reached to push
the screen open.

"You understand why I'm not comfortable talking about
Aaron and me not sleeping together, don't you?"

"Ordinarily, yeah. But the way things are, it makes me
wonder."

"You think I was so hungry for loving I led Hank on. I'll
admit I'm very fond of Hank, he's an understanding and
smart kid, but I wasn't letting him into my bed or even
teasing him, and I didn't kill Aaron so I could find a new
lover. Will you believe that?"

"I'll give it a try."

"If you help me, you won't be sorry," she said. "I didn't
do it."

I said okay and went back to Annabelle's thinking I'd
make a telephone call to Hank.

7

Back at the duplex I found Annabelle sitting by Kip in his room. His head was down and he was crying.

"What's wrong?" I asked.

Annabelle looked up with tragic eyes. "He's been beaten up—some boys at the park . . ."

I moved close and crouched before him.

"They bust your nose?" I asked.

He shook his head.

"Teeth okay?"

He nodded.

I looked at his clenched fists and saw the knuckles were unscuffed.

"How about we go have a root beer and you tell me about it?"

He shook his head.

"Come on," coaxed Annabelle, "tell Uncle Carl."

He said, "Lemme alone."

She looked at me and I nodded, patted his shoulder, and got up.

When we were in the kitchen I asked if he'd told her what happened and she said yes but she'd promised not to tell me.

"Why?"

"I can't tell you. I promised."

"He's not ashamed because he lost a fight? Everybody loses sometime."

"He doesn't believe you have, or that Hank has either. You and his father and his brother, you make him ashamed to lose or even be afraid."

So. Annabelle never found fault with her friends, but she saw family with clear eyes. I didn't try to argue with her. The truth is, I've never been able to accept the idea I lost a fight, I just got outlasted a time or two. But I sure didn't figure Kip or anybody else had to be the same as me.

I went back into his bedroom, sat on the bed beside where he'd stretched out, and told him he'd feel better if he unloaded, and if he didn't care about that, I'd feel better if he trusted me enough to talk about it. It took a while but finally I got it.

He'd been riding his bike to the park when he saw a gang of kids, maybe six or seven, on the sidewalk. He swerved to the opposite side of the road, avoiding them, but one guy hollered wait a minute and ran to cut him off. Kip wasn't sure he could get pumping fast enough to slip by, so he stopped. The kid demanded a ride. Kip pointed out his narrow handlebars and said carrying a rider wouldn't work on this bike. The kid got tough and insisted.

"He was on my left," said Kip, "and I was straddling the bike and holding the handlebars. When I shook my head he hit me on the nose. I never saw it coming. Then he hollered, 'You gonna gimme me a ride?' and I said I couldn't and hung on to the handles and he hit me again and knocked me down with the bike and called me a son of a bitch and laughed and went back to his gang."

"Well," I said, "the mistake you made was in not taking off like hell the minute he moved to cut you off."

"I was scared," he said. "This kid wasn't any bigger than me, maybe shorter but wide, you know? I figured he could lick me, and I knew if he couldn't his gang'd help. I was scared yellow."

"Come on. That was a deal no kid could fight his way out of. You showed guts just turning him down."

"You'd have taken him on the bar and ridden off a ways and beat his ears off," he said.

It shook me that this thirteen-year-old read my mind, but I said don't be silly. "It was like you told him, you couldn't carry a guy on a bike with handlebars like that."

"I could've pedaled straight far enough, and if I couldn't, he'd have seen it wouldn't work."

"Kip," I said, "just be glad those guys didn't pound you into the ground and steal the bike, okay? And nobody thinks you're a pansy because you didn't slug your way out. How's the schnozz? You breathing okay?"

"He didn't break it," he said with what sounded like regret.

"Well, you're gonna have twin shiners," I said. "If anybody cracks wise about it, tell 'em they ought to see the other guy."

He didn't try to pretend he'd ever say that, but he brightened a little and I told him he'd be okay and when he was up to it I'd show him a couple tricks he could use that had helped me if he'd promise not to use them on his brother. He'd only promise not to use them till he caught up in size some.

I went back to the kitchen and asked Annabelle if I could call long distance to Hank in Corden. She said of course, let her have a word when I was through.

The phone was in the hall, and pretty soon I had Hank on the other end. He was grateful to hear Stella was out of jail for the time being and asked what I'd found out.

"I found out she didn't like him much, the murder weapon came from her knife drawer, and half this town thinks you were making out with her. One guy told me if you weren't in Corden you'd be the prime suspect."

That brought only silence.

"Had you been making out?"

"No," he said, trying for righteous indignation, but I thought I sensed more regret than indignation.

"Had you tried?"

"Of course not!"

"Why, because she might not let you?"

"I didn't think it'd be fair to her."

"Fair? What the hell's fair in love?"

"I mean, she was so vulnerable. She'd have hated herself if she'd let me do it because she was lonely."

"You're telling me she didn't let you think you were a terrific guy?"

"Well, she let me know she liked me and all. Once she said she wished I were older. . . ."

"Yeah. Do you know if she had any other comforters?"

"She didn't have any lovers, if that's what you're trying to imply." The indignation was loud and clear this time.

"How'd you know?"

"Well, because. She didn't go anywhere and nobody came to the house."

"You kept good watch?"

"Look, if you're trying to make out she was having an affair or something and her boyfriend killed Aaron, just forget it. She didn't do it, and she wasn't involved with anybody who'd do it for her, believe me."

"Did she ever talk about leaving him?"

"Well, she couldn't do that. She didn't have any money and she loved the house and like she told me, he wasn't around enough to bother her too much. It wasn't like she hated him. It was just she was so wasted, you know?"

"When you clobbered him that night last year, how'd he act?"

"Oh, he apologized to me. I mean, he felt awful about having lost his temper and slapping Stella. He said he was grateful to me for protecting her, that I was a really wonderful guy to do it. When I apologized back he said that was just plain uncalled for and I should forget it. He'd been in the wrong and I'd done the proper thing. He even told me he appreciated my being nice to Stella and spending some time with her nights when he was off with the band because she was a very social person and got lonely. He said I could come around anytime."

So that was why he hadn't been able to make a pass. Aaron made him believe he trusted him and he couldn't be a villain and betray that trust. I began to think Aaron might have been as tricky as his wife claimed.

▽

8

AFTER ANNABELLE FINISHED talking with Hank she came into the kitchen where I was having a smoke and wanted to know why I'd called him.

"Wanted to see how Stella handled him and how he and Aaron got on after their mix-up."

"What do you mean, 'handled him'?"

"You know darned well. You wouldn't have let him go to Corden if you weren't worried about something going on with her."

She sighed, smoothed her forehead with her fingertips, and closed her eyes a moment.

"He's old for his age in ways," she said, "and Stella had a weakness for him. I won't pretend I couldn't see that. They both like poetry, you know, and she was lonely. I trusted them, but I was afraid."

"Hank says Aaron thanked him for knocking him down when he took a swing at his wife. Did you know that?"

"Yes, Aaron told me himself. He thought the world of Hank and was terribly ashamed about slapping Stella. He really was a sweet man, but he wasn't right for her."

"He ever get flirty with you?"

"Aaron?" She laughed. "Don't be silly! I almost never saw him even. He came over the morning after the fracas and talked to me, apologizing about the embarrassment I must've felt over all the goings-on at his place."

After a while I asked what she could tell me about Gene Fox, Aaron's partner in the clothing store.

"Aaron's father, Leslie, brought him in from Chicago, where he'd been a very successful salesman in a nice store. Leslie got acquainted with him, how I don't know, and was so impressed he hired him to come to Red Ford and work, and in a year he made him assistant manager. Stella told me she thought he did it to shock Aaron into showing more interest in the store, but it didn't work. Stella said Aaron was delighted. It relieved him of the worry about not doing his part to help his father's business. Aaron even went around and told Gene how grateful he was that he'd come to work for the store. And after the old man died, Aaron and Gene worked out an agreement. They've never had any problems at all."

"How's Stella feel about Gene?"

"She respects him."

Somehow that struck me as evasive.

I found the store on a corner in dead center downtown. It was narrow for a ways inside the entrance but widened toward the back. A cashier's window overlooked everything from the far right corner where a dark-eyed, black-haired young woman watched me enter. At once a tall, dark man with curly black hair and furry eyebrows that seemed to shade his deep brown eyes appeared in the aisle ahead of me. His gray suit was as unwrinkled as the window models', the tie was center perfect, and the shoes brightly shined. He saw at first glance I was an unlikely customer, but his smile was cordial and his eyes met mine directly, ignoring my wrinkled pants and open collar.

"Yessir," he said, "what can I do for you?"

"I need a pair of pants."

He had every right to say that was obvious, but he only nodded and asked did I have a color or fabric preference. I said dark and corduroy. He didn't flinch. We walked around the corner a couple steps, he took a measuring tape from a hook and checked my waist, fingered through a stack of folded slacks, and pulled out a dark gray pair. I went into the back room, put them on, and came back. He checked the waist, measured the inseam, marked the pants at the waist and bottom, and said they would be ready in the morning.

When I'd paid the cashier my two bucks and got a nickel back, I commented it was too bad about what happened to his partner.

He said it was a tragedy.

"His wife's a good friend of my sister," I said.

"Really? Who's your sister?"

I told him and his smile broadened. "Of course. A most lovely lady. Her husband, Scott, is a good customer of ours."

"You married?" I asked.

He looked startled. For a second I thought he was going to ask why I wanted to know but then the smile returned and he said no, he had not been that fortunate yet.

"I guess you'll have a new partner now."

His eyes became thoughtful. "You mean Stella Feist, I suppose."

"Uh-huh. Think she might be a more active partner?"

"That's possible," he admitted and smiled. "Who knows, maybe we'll add a women's department."

"You wouldn't mind?"

"Hey, I'd be tickled to death. There are more women in town than men, and they buy more clothes."

"What happens if Stella gets nailed for killing Aaron?"

"That'd be terrible. Who'd believe she'd do that?"

"The police. Who'd get her share of the store?"

"Well, I don't know . . ."

"You never thought about it, huh?"

He frowned, took a deep breath, and said, "All right, yes, I have. A man can't help thinking how a tragedy's going to affect him. But I don't know what'll happen. They didn't have kids and I don't know of any relatives on either side. Aaron never spoke of any—"

"Was Stella ever interested in the business?"

"Some. She used to drop in now and again and make suggestions about displays and promotion."

"Did Aaron ever do any of that?"

"Aaron left everything to me. Absolutely. His father had faith in me and that was good enough for him. He never pretended any talent for business, or any interest either."

"You ever invited to the Feists' house?"

"Oh sure. We were good friends. Anybody'll tell you that. Excuse me, but you ask a lotta questions and you seem to be getting at something about me. You working with the police?"

"Nope. Like I told you, Annabelle's a good friend of Stella's. Asked me to look in on things. I've had some experience with murders."

"I see," he said doubtfully.

"You think of anybody else who'd gain by Aaron's murder?"

"I don't like that 'anybody else.' You make me sound like a suspect."

"So offer me some alternatives. Annabelle won't settle for Stella."

He drew himself up. "No, sir, I'm not pointing the finger at anybody and I sure's hell didn't kill Aaron. I resent any accusation, implied or direct."

"Where were you Sunday night?"

"Where I always am Sunday night. At home."

"Alone?"

He stared at me a moment before saying yes. I guessed he was lying and wondered why. Either he'd been someplace he wouldn't admit to or had a visitor he meant to keep secret.

"How far do you live from the Feists?" I asked.

He looked me in the eye as he answered.

"Just across the alley."

$\bigtriangledown$

9

As I'd warned, Kip's eyes were bruised and swollen by dinner, and he ate with his head down. I tried to cheer him up by telling him how much worse I'd looked when my nose got broken by a rock from a slingshot, but it was wasted effort.

To change the subject I suggested Annabelle come along with me for a visit to the Singers. She shook her head.

"Darlene knows I'm Stella's friend. She hates Stella and wants her to hang at the very least. You'll have to find your own way to talk to her, I'm sorry."

I walked over to the Singers' with no idea how I was going to manage but figured something'd come to me.

Darlene answered the door when I knocked. She looked like a young forty and, as I expected, was anything but the frump Annabelle described. Long dark hair with reddish tints fell shining past her high cheeks and around her shoulders. The lashes were long and black, the mouth wide and warm. Tiny crow's-feet around her hazel eyes and the corners of her mouth only gave her an experienced look.

Her eyebrows rose a notch as she looked me over.

"You're not what I expected," I said.

"Oh? And what was that?"

"Somebody frumpy and about twenty-five years older. Are you really Darlene Singer?"

"I am."

"I'm Carl Wilcox. Can we talk? I'm not selling anything."

"What do you want to talk about?" She looked past my

shoulder, and I guessed she was looking for a car I might have come in.

"What I'd like to talk about is what a good-looking woman you are, but actually I'm stuck with a problem."

She leaned against the doorjamb and said, "Tell me about it."

"Are you a widow?" I asked.

"Of a kind. Why?"

"I understand you've got a grown daughter. You must've married young."

She smiled wisely. "Somebody, somewhere, has told you how far flattery can get you. But, yes, I married young, and foolishly, and he left me. Where does that leave us?"

"Okay, I'll tell you straight. I'm Annabelle Parker's brother and you probably know she's a friend of your neighbor, Stella."

"Yes, I know who she is."

"She can't believe Stella'd murder Aaron, and she's asked me to check things out because I've done some work on murders in South Dakota. So would you tell me what happened?"

She had folded her arms when she leaned against the jamb, and she pulled them a little tighter. The wise, almost flirtatious smile disappeared.

"Who does she think killed Aaron? Me? Or Carrie?"

"Annabelle's the kind who won't believe anybody she knows could kill anybody—it's got to be a stranger or it couldn't happen. I'm sure not going to try and pin it on you, but maybe you can give me a lead in some direction that'll help."

"I've told the police all I know. Isn't it up to them to work things out?"

"Yup. But sometimes they take the quick, easy way because about ninety times out of a hundred that'll be the right one, and everybody goes with experience. Maybe I'm only going through the motions, but I think a lot of Annabelle and have to do this much. I'm trying to level with you all the way."

"I must be out of my mind," she said, straightening up. "All right, come on in. We'll talk about it."

Her story was the same I'd heard twice before. She had no explanation for why Aaron had been in the house, let alone on their stairway. He had never come uninvited before, had never entered without knocking and being admitted. Yes, he had been fond of Carrie and probably talked with her more than any other adult but her mother, but she had never seen him touch Carrie, or vice versa, and she had trusted him completely.

"With Carrie," Darlene told me, "Aaron seemed as simple as she is. They were like two children. Rather sober children."

"Are there two bedrooms upstairs?" I asked.

She said yes.

"Didn't you each have your own room?" I asked.

"Yes. But there are twin beds in her room and occasionally I sleep there with her. It's not to comfort her—Carrie has no nightmares or sleeping problems. I do. Then it's nice to have her near when I'm wakeful."

"Aaron ever show any interest in you?"

"He liked me. But he didn't make any passes, if that's what you want to know. I've never known a man as innocent as Aaron. He was unreal, as a matter of fact. That's why I'm sure his wife killed him. She's a very passionate, impulsive woman. All his calm innocence must've driven her crazy. It's a wonder to me she didn't kill him long ago."

"You think she chased him across the yard and he was coming to you for help?"

"You don't think so, do you? But that makes more sense than anything else I can think of. What would you suggest?"

"No idea."

She looked at me and smiled. "No. You can't imagine a man running from a woman, especially to another woman. You'd have taken the knife away from her, wouldn't you?"

"It'd depend on how she held it."

"Huh?"

"I remember a combat sergeant telling us what you do when somebody comes at you with a knife. If he holds it in his fist, with the point down, you can block a stab with your wrist and use a hold that'll make him drop it or you break his arm. If he holds it in his fist with the point up, you can still handle it. But when he comes with the knife held straight at you, the thumb on top and the empty hand extended—run."

"I don't think you would, no matter how it was held by a woman."

I shrugged and didn't say it would depend on the woman.

"So you were in the army," she said. "Did you go to France?"

I had. Even spent a few days in Paris before I wound up in the stockade. But I didn't tell her about that.

I asked where Carrie was.

"In her room."

"Can I talk to her?"

"No. She's very shy with strangers anytime. After the murder on our steps she couldn't possibly face talking to you now. And anyway, she couldn't tell you anything about what happened. She doesn't even know, because I didn't let her out of the room until Aaron had been taken away."

"Didn't the police talk to her?"

"Yes. They upset her awfully. Tried to trick her into either admitting she stabbed him or saying I did."

Just telling me about all that upset her badly, and she said she'd appreciate it if I'd leave now.

I said okay but would it be okay for me to come around tomorrow? I wouldn't worry her about Carrie, I'd just like to talk with her.

"What about?"

"About you."

"You want to get acquainted?"

"Why not?"

"I don't think so. It wouldn't work out. I can't leave Carrie alone."

And then Carrie appeared in the doorway from the hall beside the stairway.

"Hello," she said, smiling.

Her hair was short, curly, and blond. Unlike her mother, she had a small mouth, blue eyes, and dimples. I doubted the sun had ever touched her pale cheeks.

"Can you play a mouth organ?" she asked.

"Yes."

"Aaron was going to show me how, but he died. Could you teach me?"

"He's leaving, dear," said Darlene, "he doesn't have time."

"How about tomorrow?" I suggested, looking at Darlene.

"That'd be fine," she said. "You come back tomorrow."

I introduced myself to Carrie, who curtsied and said she was pleased to meet me, then they both walked me to the door and saw me off.

Carrie's face shone with trust and warmth. Darlene's face was stiff, expressionless, and about ten years older than when she'd answered the door.

$\triangledown$

10

My OLD MAN'S Dodge was parked at the curb in front of Annabelle's when I got back, so I wasn't surprised to find Hank sitting in the living room with Kip and his mother. He greeted me with a smug grin.

"How'd you hornswoggle Elihu into letting you take the Dodge?" I asked.

"Just explained I had to come to a friend's funeral."

"You tell him you and the friend had been fighting over the guy's wife a year ago?"

He looked at his mother with a What can you expect? expression and she told me to cut the cackle, Hank was already feeling bad enough about Aaron's murder without my trying to make something of ancient history.

I said okay and suggested Hank take a hike with me. He sighed, got up, and followed me out.

The moon was a quarter and the stars at full as we walked along the sidewalk under tall elms that hid the view of both.

"If you came to help Stella," I said, "you picked a dandy time. People around here already figure she was hot for you—showing up right now won't give her any points."

"Come on, nobody believes she'd kill Aaron, that's crazy."

"You think so? It was her knife that did it, she admits that. Everybody knows she's hot tempered, and it's plain she thought Aaron was screwing girls on the road and his neighbors at home. Add to that the talk about you and her and you've got a whole mess of people thinking she did it, but most important, the cops think so. I'm not sure her own lawyer doesn't."

He took it all in and I could practically hear the wheels spinning in his head.

"I had to come," he said finally. "I really liked him, and he liked me—"

"You were nuts about her. That's why you came."

He stopped and faced me. "Okay. What can I do?"

"I need help in finding somebody else who wanted the guy dead. You've been around, every once in a while you notice what's going on. So who've we got for prospects?"

We started walking again and after a while he asked if Gene Fox would get rights to the store if Stella took the blame for Aaron's murder.

"He owns half the place because old man Feist willed it to him. I don't know who gets the other half if there are no heirs, which Gene tells me is the case. Being across the alley makes him handy as hell but murder for profit's a gambler's game, and he doesn't seem the type. There'd have to be something going on between him and Stella before he'd take a chance like that."

"How about Carrie?" asked Hank. "Maybe he came on to her too strong, she fought him off, and her mother's keeping it covered."

I shook my head. "Whoever got the butcher knife from the Feist kitchen had to be a calculating son of a bitch—too far out to be Carrie."

"Maybe Aaron went over there to fix something for them and brought the butcher knife for the job. Something happened so he tried to love her up; she got scared and grabbed the knife."

"Sure," I said, "a little before midnight they had this chicken they wanted carved up and invited him over to do the job, but he flubbed it so they ganged up and stabbed him to death."

"When there's no logical explanation there's got to be a crazy one. It wouldn't have to be the comedy you're making it."

I granted his point and we walked for a while in silence.

"The other guy with something to gain'd be Frenchy," said Hank. "Maybe he wanted to be the leader of the band."

"Yeah, I considered him. Where's he live?"

"Somewhere on the south side. I can look it up in the phone book."

We went back to Annabelle's, found the address, and drove over in the Dodge, with Hank driving. Frenchy's wife answered our knock. She was a tall, blond Swede who told us her husband was over at Max's place, so we went there.

They were in conference discussing arrangements for the coming Saturday dance in Toonerville. Max seemed happy to see Hank, but neither of them was delighted with my company.

I asked Frenchy how he got along with the cops. He bristled a little but admitted they'd been around.

"It was just routine shit," he said. "They know who did it, all right. Don't catch them putting a woman in jail without they got the case cold, even if she is out on bail."

Hank and Max talked to each other about going to the funeral the following day and getting together afterward. Hank told him he'd be heading back to Corden pretty quick after the ceremony.

Frenchy went on at me.

"The cops aren't dumb enough to believe I'd kill anybody to take over a band. Hell, I could've started my own anytime I really wanted to. I was just working to get the talent I wanted before making my move. That's all I was waiting for, not Aaron to croak."

I let him talk awhile before asking him if he knew anybody on the road or other members of the band that might've had it in for Aaron or come out ahead by killing him.

"Absolutely, positively no. Hell, Aaron was the sweetest guy you'd ever wanna meet. That was his whole trouble. He was too nice for Stella, too soft to handle dance hall operators, too easy on guys in the band. I mean, Jesus. He'd let old Doug come back from break whenever he damn pleased. I don't mind a guy getting laid during intermission, I've gone a few myself, but who needs it three times? Hell, if I murdered anybody it'd have been Gus. That old fart never got close to the beat. Ted's damned near as bad. There were lotsa times I'd've killed them both if I was a killing man."

Eventually we left Max's place and I asked Hank if he knew where Doug the trumpet man lived.

He did and we went around in the Dodge, pulled up in front of a small white bungalow, and walked up to the porch where Doug sat on a chain-hung bench, drinking beer and swinging gently.

He was friendly enough to Hank and offered us both beers. I accepted, Hank shook his head.

Doug's hair was blond and flopped across his forehead the way guys leave it so girls will want to brush it back for them. His voice was soft and gentle as a loving touch, and when he lit a cigarette I could see the horn-blower's callus on his upper lip and the bright blue of his eyes.

"You come back for the funeral?" he asked Hank, and said that was nice when he nodded.

I asked him my routine questions and he spoke of Aaron with the same half-awe for his purity and sweet nature that the other bandsmen had shown. It would have been pretty boring if I hadn't begun to get suspicious of the consistency. I asked him if the band would be better off under Frenchy.

"It might make more money," he said, "but it won't be as much fun. Frenchy thinks he's God. I doubt I'll stick with him long."

"You gonna start a band of your own?" asked Hank.

"No, I'll maybe go to the cities, either find a better band or if that doesn't work out, get a job. I got a cousin doing real good selling stuff to chicks he stops on the street. He calls it stemming. They stop pairs of girls or even three or more and say they've got this neat special offer and set up a date for an evening at their place and pitch pots and pans. You can make good money and get laid a lot. That's better than

spending half your life in a goddamn crowded car with six
guys going and coming from dances all hours of the night."

It was past nine by the time we left Doug and I decided to
try talking with Ted, the piano man, but his landlady told
us he was over at the Eastside with Ed West, the sousaphonist. She didn't know where, but Hank guessed it'd be Jacob's.
Since he was underage I took him home and went across the
river alone, driving the Dodge, which Hank gave up reluc-
tantly.

Willie greeted me once more with his big grin, and when
I asked if Ed West and Ted Ford were around, he pointed out
the bandsmen in a booth across the room. One was a tall,
skinny guy with sandy hair, a long nose, and matching chin.
Willie said he was the sousaphonist. The stubby balding guy
across from him with the wide mouth and sad eyes was the
piano player, Ted.

I walked over, introduced myself, and sat down next to Ed
West, the tall one.

Ted gave me a sour once-over and said, "I know that name.
You're the snakeman old Willie always used to talk about.
The cowboy and bar fighter."

I confessed that pretty well summed up the story.

"What's going to happen to the band now?" I asked.

"It'll die," said Ted.

I looked at Ed. He stared back, gloomily.

"Others think Frenchy'll take over," I said.

"What's it to you?" Ted wanted to know.

"I'm nosy. Like to check out what's going on. Either of
you guys know Stella at all?"

"What do you mean, 'know'?" asked Ted. "You talkin' in
the biblical sense?"

"No. I just wonder if you guys think she could've killed
Aaron?"

"Hell no," said Ted.

"Why not?"

"Why should she? She had the house she wanted, had
good money coming in from the store she didn't have to

worry about, a husband who was gone two to three nights a week so she could screw around with anybody she liked. Why in the world would she want to mess any of that up?"

"What about their fights?"

"A lot of nothing. Now and then Stella got bored and raised a little hell just to liven things up. It shook Aaron some, but he didn't lose any sleep over it—hell, he probably thought it meant she cared."

"Somebody killed him."

"Well, yeah, there is that."

I looked at Ed. "What do you think?"

"Stella."

"You guys don't agree, then. What's your notion?"

"Aaron was in love. He never was before, but he got that way a few months back."

"Who?"

His long face seemed to get longer. "I dunno."

"Everybody keeps telling me Aaron was an innocent," I said. "You guys traveled with him, worked together. Did he mess around with the hangers-on, or do you think he had a hard-on for his simple neighbor, Carrie?"

He shrugged.

"Ed's got a thing about people in love," his short partner told me. "Says it shows in their eyes. I think it's more that he can smell it."

We talked through a couple beers without them coming up with anything more substantial, so I said good night and went back to Annabelle's and bed.

11

Kɪᴘ ᴡᴀs ɴᴏʀᴍᴀʟʟʏ the first one up, so when he hadn't
shown by the time his mother had breakfast under way, she
suggested I go check on him. He was on his back, staring at
the ceiling when I tapped on the door, then walked in. His
eyes were puffy and the swelling was black and blue.

"You're gonna need a solid breakfast," I told him. "Today
I show you a few things."

He rolled his head an inch on the pillow and asked, "Like
what?"

"Well, not how to whip your brother."

"I don't care about that anymore."

"Good. Come on down. Your ma's making waffles. When
you're all fueled up I'll show some stuff you need to know."

He didn't exactly snap to, but he was sitting up on the
edge of the bed when I left him.

Hank was standing by the window watching Stella
puttering in her vegetable garden next door as I entered the
kitchen.

He looked at me.

"You think I'd be making things worse for her if I went
over to talk?" he asked.

"What'll you talk about?"

He glanced at his mother, who was pouring batter into the
waffle iron.

"I don't know—tell her how sorry I am, I suppose."

"She might not be impressed. She told me she wasn't sorry
he was dead."

His face registered shock, then skepticism. "How could she say that?"

"To make people think she was honest."

Hank started toward the door.

"Don't give her advice," I said.

He paused, frowned, and went out.

Stella, who had been examining her young tomato plants, heard the screen door slam behind Hank, looked our way, and straightened up. Her smile, I guessed, lifted Hank's soul and maybe something more basic. He walked carefully to the garden and halted at its edge. I couldn't hear them, but neither seemed to have any trouble finding words.

I turned to Annabelle and asked if she'd ever seen a more cheerful new widow.

"She's not cheerful," said Annabelle, "she's just putting on a brave face."

They were still chinning when Kip showed up. Once she had his breakfast served, Annabelle went back to watching the garden scene while I explained the basics of self-preservation to Kip, like keep your head down and your hands high.

I promised we'd go out back later and I'd show him how to duck, which was the handiest thing to know that I could teach him in his mother's presence. One day I'd tip him off on learning to use anything handy as a weapon. I didn't figure I could get by with suggesting he use clubs or sharp instruments while his mother was listening.

The funeral that afternoon drew a crowd almost as big as a Saturday night fight in the Corden dance hall. Stella showed up, completely transformed from the gardener of that morning. Her black dress, silk stockings, and low-heeled shoes made her look like a mourning widow from the shoulders down. Above the neck it was a different story. Her eyes were too bright, her cheeks too rosy; her hair was fixed for a party, and her mouth looked more sexy than sad. I heard a few indignant mutterings here and there.

If you didn't already know different you'd have thought from the eulogy that Aaron had been the apple of God's eye, the greatest bandleader since Sousa, and a dream husband. I kept wishing Aaron's band were playing the music instead of the organist, who should have been handling a hoe, not a pipe organ. And it would have been nice if they'd had a soloist or quartet doing something by George Gershwin or the like. Instead we had a choir and hymns. From the reactions of the mob flowing out of the church after the service, it'd been a beautiful, enriching experience, so it seemed like everybody but me got what they wanted.

I tried to spot any cops in attendance but recognized none, and no one in the crowd looked guilty or suspicious any way I could spot. All the band showed up along with their fans. Darlene Singer was there with Carrie, who kept her head lowered except when Darlene greeted me on the sidewalk. Then the young woman gave me a sudden, out-of-place bright smile and asked when I'd teach her the mouth organ.

That flustered Darlene, who seemed even more upset when I said how about in half an hour at their house.

"Aren't you going to the cemetery?" she asked, making it sound like an accusation.

"Nope. I think they can manage that without me. You going?"

"No," said Carrie, "Mama says enough is enough."

Darlene's eyes rolled. She took a deep breath and said, all right, they'd expect me in a bit, but make it an hour.

I looked around before leaving and saw Stella in the midst of sympathizers. She had managed to make her mouth corners droop, but it only added to her sexiness.

Hank went on to the cemetery in a car with friends, and I walked Annabelle home.

"I appreciate what you're trying to do with Kip," she said, "but it might be better if you just let him alone."

"Why?"

"I remember when his father talked with Hank after Hank was bullied by some boy at the fair. He told him don't wait for the other fellow to start something; if he gives you trouble just hit him on the nose. And the very next day Hank hit the Olson boy and gave him a terrible nosebleed and Mrs. Olson hasn't spoken to us since."

"Come on, sis, you told me that one long ago, and Hank was only six when he did that. Kip's older, and besides I'm not telling him to start a fight, I'm trying to help him handle a scrap when he can't get out of it."

"Carl, he's not like you, and it'll probably never in his life happen again that some bully'll stop him and hit him. You and Scott are fellows that invite trouble. You know it, you both glory in it, and I'd like Kip to be one boy in our family who really grows up."

"You think Hank hasn't?"

"Yes, but that's not because of his father or uncle, he did it on his own."

That got me where the skin is thin, since I'd seen Hank's attitudes switch from something near hero worship to accepting the disapproval of me, encouraged by his grand-parents when he started going through high school.

So when I went in the backyard with Kip I only taught him ducking, a hammerlock, and the flying mare. I skipped choke holds, high kicks, and a knee to the family jewels. Hank had already taught him the old reliable hip throw. He got the ideas pretty fast and liked my laying on the advantages a smaller fighter has if he moves fast enough and on target.

"Being lower, you've got the leverage," I told him. "But never forget, if the other guy's really big, you don't gain anything being on the bottom if he can get all his weight on you. The flying mare works when you use his height and heft to keep him moving the way he started. You only get him up to get him over and down fast as you can. And hang on to his arm all the way. You don't let go of a hammer when it's just going to hit the nail."

At first he was pretty glum and slow, but as I made him practice putting on a hammerlock and actually got him to throw me once, he did okay. He was very quick, and when I gave a really good grunt the last time he threw me he couldn't hide his excitement.

I told him to find a good friend to bring over who was his size and we'd work up a routine. When he went in the house his face was bright in spite of the black eyes.

I was late getting over to the Singers', and Darlene frowned at me when she opened the door.

"Did you bring a harmonica?" she asked.

I said no.

"Well, that's too bad. Carrie seems to have misplaced hers. She has a talent for losing things. When she does she gets very embarrassed. She's hiding now, up in her room."

"Okay, how about you and I talk?"

"About what?"

"Aaron. How'd he happen to start helping you with household chores and problems?"

She frowned thoughtfully. "I'm really not sure. I guess we just got talking one afternoon when he'd been cutting his lawn and I was weeding the garden. I admitted I'd had trouble finding someone to do odd jobs around the house. Boys I'd hired were either irresponsible and stupid or they got too interested in Carrie. Young boys learn fast how susceptible she is and try to get her alone so they can feel her and, you know. . . ."

"So Aaron volunteered to be your handyman?"

"I guess it came down to that. He was a sweet man."

"What were you and Carrie doing when you heard the noises on the stairway?"

"Well, I'd been reading Carrie a book of fairy tales, and when I was through I heard something and told Carrie to listen. Then there was the cry and a loud thump and then louder ones. Carrie was terrified and I held her until the noises stopped and well beyond. We were petrified."

"Were there any chores Aaron promised to do that he hadn't gotten around to? Wasn't there some reason you could figure why he came to be on your steps?"

She looked back down the hall behind her, turned back to me, pushed the screen open, and stepped outside.

"Let's go around to the garden," she said.

We went side by side and I saw her glancing about to see if we were observed. In back she had two rattan chairs by the rear door and waved me into one as she sat in the other.

"I guess it's only fair to be honest with you, Carl. I'm afraid Aaron wasn't entirely an angel. He fell in love with Carrie. I was honest when I told you they seemed like two children together, but they were both affectionate and I began to realize something was happening I couldn't control. It's pretty obvious to me now that somehow, some way, he persuaded Carrie that he should visit her in her room. That night he was coming to join her. I think she was afraid and that's why she asked me to read the fairy tales that night and stay with her. She had never done that before."

"And you think Stella followed him when he sneaked out and caught him halfway up?"

"Of course. What else could've happened?"

▽

12

STELLA WAS IN the kitchen with Annabelle when I got back. The glow she'd had during the funeral was gone. She watched my eyes while Annabelle told me the police were waiting when Hank returned from the cemetery, and they took him to the station.

"Have you called Hamilton?" I asked.

Annabelle's hand rose to her face. "You think he needs a lawyer?"

"Yeah," I said and went to the phone.

Hamilton said, "Damn!" when I told him what was up. "Was it your idea for that young idiot to come here now?"

"No. Are you going to try and get him out?"

"I don't like it. Scott isn't home, is he?"

"Look, you don't need his daddy's okay to bail out his kid. You want me to go with you to the station?"

"No, sir. Absolutely not. I've already heard mutterings from the police about your poking about in this case, and they don't like it. Tell Annabelle I'll talk to her later."

Stella and Annabelle went on about it for a while after I joined them in the kitchen again. Stella was all apologies for getting Hank into this mess, and of course Annabelle comforted her with heart and soul, assuring her she couldn't take the blame and all would be well.

Hank showed up shortly after Stella went home. It was plain his session with the cops had rattled him. He sat at the kitchen table hardly picking at food he'd normally clear off so fast the plate hardly needed washing. I'd called him hollow legs since he was four because of his appetite. It gradually came out that they'd worked the old good-cop, bad-cop routine with one accusing him of screwing the neighbor's wife and being involved in the stabbing, while the other tried to convince him that he understood how a young man would fall for such an attractive woman and innocently get involved in a tragic affair. I guessed that he'd given neither one of them any satisfaction by the time Al Hamilton showed up and put a stop to it all.

They had worked hard to make him suspicious of Stella and tried to convince him they knew of other men she'd messed with. They kept bringing up Gene Fox. Mostly that just made Hank mad, but I sensed they'd planted doubts in his mind he couldn't quite shake off.

And they told him flat not to leave town.

Before dinner he telephoned his grandfather and explained why he couldn't bring the Dodge back for a few days. If I'd made such a call Elihu's reaction would've melted the wires, but of course he just told Hank not to worry, he could get along fine. What galled me most was it never for a moment occurred to Hank that his grandfather wouldn't accept what happened just the way he did.

Annabelle grinned at me and made some crack about how Hank had a way with older folks.

After dinner I went out back and was rolling a smoke when Stella pushed open her screen door and walked toward her vegetable garden. She'd changed from the funeral black into a dark blue housedress and flat shoes but still looked smart.

I was almost at her side before she noticed me, started slightly, and managed a smile.

"You walk like a cat," she said.

"Who spaded over your garden in spring?" I asked.

She faced me square and wrinkled her brow delicately.

"What a strange question. I did it myself. Who'd you think?"

"I didn't figure Aaron, thought maybe Hank."

"He wasn't here. But he did do it the spring before. What're you getting at?"

"Just trying to get the whole picture. You don't seem like

a woman who'd garden at all, let alone do the heavier work."

"Most women are more than men ever imagine. I don't mind using a spade or a fork, although I'll admit I've never worked with a pickax or sledgehammer, but then, I never needed them for the gardening. Have you ever cooked?"

"Sure."

"Okay. And that doesn't surprise me. I bet you're good at anything you try, and I'd guess you'd try anything."

She turned from me and examined the garden critically.

"I should hoe some, but I don't feel like it. You know what I'd dearly love to do?"

"Go over to the Eastside?"

She started to laugh, squelched it, glanced quickly toward Annabelle's house, then the street, and finally sighed.

"Yes. You see right through me. I'd love to go there and play some slot machines and dance. Do you dance?"

"Not much."

"That's too bad. Tell me, Carl, what have you learned about me in talking with people? I'm dying to know what they say, really. They think I killed Aaron, don't they?"

"Some do."

"What do you think?"

"I think no."

"Because Annabelle believes in me?"

"Nope. I don't think you'd have done it that way."

"You didn't think I'd spade my own garden, either."

"True."

"You think I'm cool and calculating. That I married Aaron because I thought he'd be somebody and hated him for being a lousy musician but didn't have the fire to stab him. Does that sum it up?"

"It's warped some."

She gave a bitter laugh, crouched down, and pruned a small tomato sideshoot with her thumbnail. "What've you found out about Aaron? Who was he making love to?"

"Nobody seems to know. I'd guess a guy that didn't want you just wasn't much interested in women."

She stood up and glanced toward the onion sets.

"It needs watering. Everything always needs watering in this damned country." She turned back to me again. "How'd you guess he wasn't interested in me?"

"A lot of things. Like him being gone so much and not doing what you wanted about the store."

"That's not the half of it. I told you Aaron and I hadn't made love in years, didn't I?"

"You said ten."

"Yes, well, it wasn't much when we did it anyway, so I didn't really care at first. I never expected trips to the stars and all that romantic stuff. If I hadn't read a lot of stupid books maybe I'd never have cared, I don't know."

The glow was back in her face and she stood with her head slightly bent, looking down as she rubbed the thumbnail she'd cut the tomato plant with.

"What'd you do about all that?" I asked.

"Nothing," she said. "I bought furniture and cleaned house, worked my garden and repainted some rooms. And in the past couple years I've daydreamed of seducing Hank but couldn't quite come down to it because of Annabelle." She looked at me. "And you know what? I really don't think she'd have condemned me for it if I had. She's just the most understanding, wonderful woman I've ever known. But I think she'd have been disappointed in me. Somehow I couldn't bear disappointing Annabelle."

I guessed I'd done that pretty regular, but it didn't seem worth mentioning.

She continued looking at the garden, then she started talking again.

"I want you to believe I didn't kill him. I don't know how I can convince you, but somehow I must. Will you come over and see me later? After dark when nobody will see?"

It didn't seem real smart, but of course I said sure. What time?

She said eleven.

13

SHE WAS STILL wearing the blue housedress and flat shoes when she let me in the back door. We walked through the unlit kitchen to the parlor, where a small lamp on top of an old upright piano threw deep shadows. The blinds were drawn tight to the sill on all the windows.

We sat side by side on a sagging couch, and she began talking in a nervous rush.

"I was an only child. My mother was forty when she had me, too old for it, you see, and died in labor. I lived with her older sister till she got senile when I was almost through high school. Her husband died in a fall from a silo he was helping build. Nobody ever told me anything about my father, but it's pretty plain my mother hadn't been married to him. I always told myself, when I learned about such things, that she'd been raped. But I don't really know. My aunt just told me she was a dear sweet woman with not enough religion and very bad luck. She let me know that's what happened if you didn't have religion. It seems to me a very strange view of things now, but I believed it then. I went to Sunday school and summer bible school and church when I was big enough. I still go because that's what a woman does, and I'm afraid of getting bad luck."

A friend of my aunt's took a fancy to her and bought her a beautiful dress she could wear to parties. It was silk and deep blue, but there were no parties to wear it to so her aunt let her wear it to school. At first the children were awed and then offended, but she kept wearing it until it wasn't pretty anymore and kids made fun of her.

During her last year in high school she was a live-in maid for a neighbor of her aunt, and she joined the church choir and became a soloist. "The director had a case on me because I could sing either soprano or alto. You know who he was?"

I shook my head and she said, "Aaron. He was about five years older than me, the son of a very prominent business-man. I thought I was in love with him from the start. We got married, and when he first started his band I went along as their singer. I didn't get paid anything but I didn't care. It was fun and I felt important. All the fellows in the band made a big thing of taking turns holding me in their laps because Aaron always drove, so I couldn't sit in his and there wasn't room for all of us unless I doubled. That got old in a hurry. And nobody at a dance pays any attention to the singer except some nasty fellows who tried to get me out in cars during intermissions."

She thought at least one other guy in the band should drive his car so they'd have some room, but nobody wanted to pay for the extra expense. Finally she said she'd quit if they didn't, and they still didn't so she kept her word.

"And nobody cared," she said. "I was never missed that I know of, not even by Aaron. I've never sung since. Not a note."

"Can you play that piano?"

"Sure."

"Sing me one of your favorites."

"You're kidding."

"No."

"You really want me to?"

"Why'd I ask if I didn't?"

"The piano's probably out of tune," she said, but she got to her feet, went over, pulled the small dark stool out, and sat down. "My voice is probably rusty."

"Got anything to drink?"

She laughed. "Yes, there's some whiskey in the kitchen cabinet, under the sink."

I offered to get it but she said no, she didn't want to turn the light on, and only she could find it. I stood by the piano, waiting until she returned with two glasses and handed me one. She hadn't bothered with ice or mix.

"Cheers," she said, and took a swallow.

I felt the glow down to my belly. I watched her set her glass on the piano top, touch her fingers and thumbs together, and press lightly, stretching her hands before she lowered them to the keys to run a string of notes. Then she started playing, and I recognized "I'm Dancing with Tears in My Eyes." She sang it through and repeated the chorus, then went into "Melancholy Baby," "Mary," and finally "Goodnight Ladies." Her voice was husky on low notes, soft on the higher ones, and nice on them all. She wasn't that good on the piano playing and had the bad amateur's habit of correcting missed notes.

She stopped abruptly, saying she was awful.

I told her there was nothing wrong with her singing.

She swiveled on the chair so her knees almost touched mine and smiled up.

"You're really very nice, Carl."

She seemed embarrassed. She looked at my left hand and reached for it.

"You have very good hands," she said. "Strong looking, but not gross. Do you like my hands?"

I told her they were great.

"You're not much of a romancer, are you?"

I put my empty glass on the piano, took her by the elbows, and brought her up. She closed her eyes and lifted her face to meet mine.

She didn't speak when I picked her up and carried her to the bedroom. She offered no help as I undressed her. I lay down at her side and began hugs and kisses, but while she kissed back her body was stiff and afraid.

"I'm no good at this," she said.

She wasn't. She said no when I moved too quickly once, so I took lots of time. There was no more resistance than there was help. All she wanted was to be taken gently—it didn't occur to her she could give anything. I hinted once it'd be okay for her to move and she managed a twitch or two, more out of politeness than sociability. Forget about passion.

I tried rolling over and having her on top but that didn't liven things up, so finally I did my thing missionary style and then we lay awhile side by side and she said she hoped it was okay, and I said she was terrific and she cried.

That got me so sad for her I wanted to try again, thinking maybe it would go somewhere, but the notion seemed to scare her. All at once she was pulling on clothes and saying I really ought to go and be careful nobody saw me.

▽

14

AFTER BREAKFAST FRIDAY morning, Kip went off and came back with his friend, Lenny Krueger. Lenny was half a thought shorter than Kip, a hint wider, and wore a thoughtful, worried look. I led them out back and we started work on wrestling holds and throws. Right away it was plain they liked each other too well to work at being top dog, so I could concentrate on the teaching and not worry about them hurting each other or getting mad. Before long they were grass stained, scuffed up, and having a great time.

"The best part of a good workout in North Dakota," I told them, "is you don't get all sweaty." That didn't impress them since they were natives and didn't know the meaning of humidity.

We sat on the ground awhile as they got their breath. Kip asked if I'd build him a chinning bar like the one I'd made his brother some years back.

"Would you use it?"

"Sure. So'd Lenny."

I said it was a deal. We drove downtown in my Model T and bought pipe, cement, and gravel and hauled it back home. While I was digging the holes with a borrowed posthole digger, Hank came around looking sour and asked questions that made it plain he was suspicious about where I'd spent the night before. I figured out he'd seen me talking with Stella in her garden just before he left to join his buddy Max.

His sourness increased when his questions got no answers

that suited him. Finally he said he'd heard her piano when he came home from Max's, and it surprised him because he'd not heard it in a few years.

I kicked the yellow clay off the posthole digger and gave him a sideways squint.

"Maybe you should've knocked on her door and checked it out. I imagine she'd be real thrilled you were interested."

He looked at the two kids sitting near and taking all this in with wide eyes.

"Why don't you guys go in the kitchen and ask Mom if you can have some lemonade?" he said.

Kip looked at me.

"Go ahead. See if she'll let you bring us some."

Lenny liked the idea and got to his feet. Kip slowly followed suit, and they moved off.

"Well," said Hank, "were you over there?"

"I was."

"Is that how you're gonna prove she didn't kill her husband?"

"That's right. I figured if she could play the piano well enough, folks'd know she couldn't do anything like stab her husband with a butcher knife."

"I don't believe that."

"You mean you think she stabbed him?"

His face twisted and suddenly he squatted down, then sat, as if his legs were too weak to hold him. I put the digger aside and sat opposite him with my legs folded tailor fashion.

"The police are positive," he said. "They say she's a passionate, hot-tempered woman who caught her man messing around, and killed him. They say she can probably claim she was crazy, so she won't go to prison, just to someplace where they'll take care of her and make sure she doesn't hurt anybody else."

"You think they're right?"

"I know she loses her temper and it made her really mad that Aaron'd fool with Carrie. She thought it was degrading and that's why he did it, because he knew he wasn't good enough for Stella, so he wanted somebody with a mind like a little girl."

"I don't think Stella did it," I said.

For a second his eyes lit up, then his doubts returned.

"You're just saying that."

I shook my head. "I don't believe a woman who loses her temper and hits her man with her hands suddenly goes nuts and tries to make him a sieve with a butcher knife. Especially not in the neighbors' house. I don't see it."

"But who else?"

"I'm working on it."

"By building a chinning bar for Kip?"

"That's not part of it, no. Neither is eating at mealtime or sleeping at night, but I do that stuff and I'm going to keep on doing it. Okay?"

"I'm not in love with her," he said, not looking at me. "I thought I was when I tackled Aaron. If he'd really been beating her, like had a club or something, I guess I'd have tried to kill him. But later, when he was so nice about it, I felt awful. I suppose maybe I do love her in a way, but she never really cared any about me."

"She admitted to me last night she wanted to seduce you. She held off because she thought it'd make Annabelle mad at her."

I wasn't sure it was smart to tell him that, but he brightened up so strong I couldn't regret it.

"She really said that?"

"Yeah. She's a hell of a good-looking woman, you know. You don't have to be ashamed about wanting her just because she's some older."

"I'm not ashamed. I was when Aaron was alive because I knew it wasn't right, wanting his wife."

"You didn't maybe wheel back here last weekend and do him in, did you?"

"That's not funny," he said as Kip and Lenny came out the back door, each carrying two tall glasses of lemonade.

Hank drifted off after his drink. I finished building the

chinning bar and told Kip to stay off it until Saturday, when I could be sure the concrete base was dry.

Stella didn't show up in her garden through the afternoon, but I thought I saw her looking out the kitchen window a time or two. I figured she was wondering what I'd told Hank. She probably thought she knew men well enough to think I couldn't resist bragging.

Scott, Annabelle's husband, got home a little before supper, parked out front in his shiny new Model A just behind my grubby old Model T, and came up to the house wearing his blue-and-white striped seersucker suit, a red and blue tie on a white shirt, and black and white shoes. It was all topped off by a straw skimmer perched at a cocky angle. He was so spiffy I couldn't help thinking about dousing him with the hose.

I'd been sitting on the porch swing flanked by Kip and Hank when he drove up. They both slipped off to meet him, and I couldn't help thinking they didn't want to be seen too close to a man as scruffy as me when their snazzy dad was home.

Scott never pretended he was tickled pink to see me but was polite and shook hands hard enough to make sure I hadn't gone soft since we last met. He handed his bag to Kip, who carried it inside to search for the magazines usually stacked on top, and after polite noises to me hurried in to find Annabelle.

Hank went with him while I sat down to roll a smoke and think. That's never much agreed with me, so I got up and walked around back to inspect the chinning bar, which was still straight and looked the right height.

Stella was on her knees weeding her garden. When she saw me she sat on her heels and tipped her head back. I walked over.

"What've you told Hank?" she asked. She tried to sound casual but it came out tight.

"I told him you didn't murder Aaron."

That seemed to surprise her, because some of the tension left her jaw as she managed a bitter smile.

"Did you tell him I wasn't passionate enough?"

I told her exactly what I'd said to Hank.

She lowered her head and her shoulders sagged. "Thank you. I believe you and I'm truly grateful. I wish it could be left at that. I don't really want to know who killed Aaron, or even why. I just want it forgotten. Isn't that weird?"

"No."

"I wish I'd been better for you," she said. "I could promise to be different another time but I probably wouldn't be. I'm grateful you were so . . . understanding.

Her gratitude was beginning to wear on me, and I couldn't quite make myself offer to give it another try soon. Then Annabelle saved the situation by calling me to supper.

▽

15

FRIDAY NIGHT SCOTT took Annabelle to a dance at the Legion hall. I went over to the Eastside, thinking partly of beer, a little of women, and not much about the murder.

Willie greeted me when I bellied up to Jacob's bar and asked if I'd had any good fights lately. I said no and he shook his head and told me I was growing old.

"Well, it's easier than growing young."

I talked some with a bottle blond barfly who lost interest when I didn't accept her offer for private entertainment at a price. During that proposition I noticed in the mirror a short, middle-aged guy at a booth with a woman who could only have been his wife. They kept watching me; she seemed to be egging him into something.

I was working on my second beer when he showed up at my elbow and said, "Excuse me."

"For what?" I asked.

He grinned and said, "For intruding on your privacy."

"I don't come to a bar for privacy. What can I do for you?"

His grin broadened, stretching his gray mustache and half closing his eyes. "We, my wife and I, would like to talk to you, Mr. Wilcox. It's a confidential matter." He gave the bartender's broad back a significant glance and tilted his head toward the booth he'd left.

It didn't sound exciting but talking to my beer was no thrill, and it was nice to find a stranger who knew my name and still wanted to talk with me. I picked up my glass, slipped off the stool, and walked back to meet his wife.

She was plumped up as a new pillow and watched our approach with a smile that dimpled her plump cheeks and showed off good store teeth. She held a cigarette between the tips of her thumb and forefinger and took shy puffs now and again while taking in everything around her.

"This is Gertrude," said my sudden host. "I'm Milo Perkins. I used to be a salesman for Feist's Haberdashery in Red Ford."

He sat beside his wife. I slid in across from them, placing my glass of beer on the table. She asked if they could buy me a drink. I thanked her and said the beer'd hold me.

"I was here," said Milo, "the time you had the snake wrapped around your middle under your jacket several years ago. It almost made a teetotaler out of me. You don't happen to have the snake around you tonight?"

"She died."

"A pity. Well, I happened to notice you a couple nights ago and got talking with Willie, who told me you're Annabelle's brother. I know she's very close to Stella. I guess you know Stella's husband was half owner of Feist's Haberdashery?"

I nodded and drank some beer. He cradled his glass affectionately with both hands, as if to warm it. His wife was propped cozily in her corner, watching us as if we were two favorite grandchildren.

"Mr. Fox inherited half-interest in the store when Aaron's father died," Milo told me. "He's managed it ever since."

"So I've heard."

"He's an ambitious man." He said that as if he wanted it to sound respectable but actually wasn't quite convinced.

I began to roll a cigarette. He glanced toward the bar, caught Willie's eye, and raised his glass to signal for a refill. He looked at me again.

"Like I said, I worked at the store. Many years. The first Mr. Feist hired me himself and treated me like a son. I met Gertrude in the store. She was the bookkeeper. We got married and Mr. Feist gave us a two-week paid vacation for our honeymoon. When he died and Mr. Fox took over, everything changed. We expected that, of course, but nothing like what happened. Mr. Fox was nice at first, but early on we realized he resented Aaron having half-interest and not doing anything for the store. Gertrude could see it in the way he reacted every time he had to sign the check for Aaron's share of the sales. He about ground his teeth. And when Aaron came around, which wasn't often, Mr. Fox'd glare at him when his head was turned and even made sarcastic remarks about him being so interested in the store's business."

When his drink was delivered, he took a good swallow before lowering it to the table and cradling it again.

"Then he started complaining about Gertrude's bookkeeping. He didn't like her system and said she made mistakes. One day he gave her a week's notice and let her go. I wanted to quit then, but Gertrude made me stay because of course we needed the money and other sales jobs weren't that handy. Pretty soon he was complaining that I didn't know how to deal with young people and that my ideas about clothing were old and my customers weren't buying enough good things. He was partly right, of course. I had a great bunch of loyal customers in the old days, then gradually they died off, moved away, or retired; they didn't need many clothes anymore. The young customers have no loyalty. They don't listen to you or even look at you, just grab what they want and buy it. So finally I got a job with Eckerson's Clothing and took a great deal of pleasure in telling Mr. Fox I was quitting."

"How'd he take it?"

"He was very pleasant, as a matter of fact. He said maybe it'd be good for me. A man should never get into ruts no matter how old he gets."

I decided to have another beer and moved to get it but Milo said please, let him, so I sat back and watched as he went to the bar with my glass.

"I guess," said Gertrude, "you're wondering why Milo's been going into all this?"

"Some," I admitted.

"He knows your sister brought you from South Dakota to try and keep Stella from taking blame for Aaron's death. Most everybody interested in the store knows that. We don't believe Stella'd kill her husband. Milo thinks Mr. Fox's the one. He can't quite bring himself to tell you that, but he wants you to look into it."

"Has he said anything to the cops?"

"No. He's positive they'll just think he's an unhappy former employee who carries a grudge because Mr. Fox fired me."

"Was there anything to Fox's complaints about your work?"

"Well, would you think I'd have a purely impartial view of that?"

"I guess not."

She smiled. "For what it's worth, I'll tell you his complaints were made up—I've been working at the bank since I left the store and've never had any criticism of my work. You can check that easily."

"Okay. Who's been handling bookkeeping for Feist's since you left?"

"I understand Mr. Fox does it personally."

"So you think he jockeyed the books and shortchanged his partner?"

Milo returned with my beer and slipped in beside Gertrude once more. He had heard my last comment and his eyes were bright.

"It makes sense, doesn't it?" he said.

"Maybe. But if he was getting away with that, he wouldn't have any good reason to knock off Aaron, would he?"

"Sure. He'd still be paying out a good deal. Who knows, maybe Aaron suspected he was being shorted and asked for an audit."

"Or maybe Stella figured that out," I suggested.

"She might have. You know, she used to come into the store and talk with Mr. Fox in his office. I heard him thank her once for her ideas about window displays and advertising. He played up to her real strong."

"I think you ought to tell the police about this."

Gertrude sighed and looked at her husband.

"No. Milo's afraid he'd get called on to testify and he just won't do it. What's worse, he thinks it just might make things tougher for Stella since there's already been some talk about her being cozy with Mr. Fox."

"You bet your sweet life," said Milo. "I know how those lawyers crucify a man on the witness stand. I don't want any of that."

We were quiet a moment as we tried our drinks. Then Milo lifted his head and asked if I'd talked to Fox. I said yes.

"Did he tell you what he was doing Sunday night?"

"He said he was home alone."

"Could he prove it?"

I shook my head.

"You know where he lives, don't you?"

"Yeah, right behind Stella's house. You got anything else?"

"You know about Biddy Swenson?"

I shook my head.

"She worked for Mr. Fox. Handled the phones and did some of the record keeping for customers. She had a tiff with him and he canned her. I never heard exactly what that was about, but she could have heard things or maybe noticed the business was doing better than Mr. Fox wanted Aaron to know. You might talk to her."

"She in town?"

"No. She married a guy from Clifton. That's west of here."

"What's her married name?"

"Swenson. His name's Pete. He works in his old man's grocery store there."

I thanked them for the beer and conversation and went back to the bar. They left a few minutes later. A little after eleven, when things were getting quiet, I asked Willie about them.

"They're okay. He give you a story on Gene Fox?"

"Yeah. Is he a liar?"

"No. You can believe him. He's an old-fashioned honest guy. Not many of us left. He tell you that him and Gertrude figure Stella did in Aaron?"

"Not exactly. Is that what *you* think?"

"Sure. Everybody does."

$\triangledown$

16

LATE SATURDAY MORNING the sun blazed down, making me squint till my face ached as I raised a spiraling trail of yellow dust on the graveled road to Clifton. It seemed sure if I met some other damn fool along the way, we'd both suffocate.

The town was quiet as a country school house in July when I drove into the heart of it and angle-parked against a high concrete curb in front of a grocery store with a sun-faded sign that said it was Swenson's Market.

I got down from the car, hitched up my pants, and went inside. It was a little dark after the blinding sunshine and smelled of fresh apples and sweeping compound. A lanky dude behind the counter at left center raised his head, took me in, and nodded a good morning. A stout woman custo-mer stood by, watching him add up her account. Her eyes didn't leave his pad.

I wandered past an apple bin, picked out a solid red one, and drifted over to the counter as the lady counted out her quarters, dimes, and pennies. She gave me a suspicious glance, picked up her bag of groceries, and left.

The lanky man accepted my nickel for the apple, glanced out at my car, and asked how the sign painting business was.

"Not so sure as the grocery business. I notice your sign's a little tired. I could wake it up in no time, make it better than new."

"How much?"

I told him.

He frowned and I said, "Okay, how about you pay off in groceries?"

"I'll have to talk with Pa. He owns the place."

"Fine. You want a special sign for the window? Feature for the day?"

"Not likely. You want groceries around here, this is the only place to come."

"Okay, so we do the big sign for pride, right?"

"I like the idea," he admitted, "but Pa decides."

While I chewed my apple another housewife came in and started telling Swenson what she wanted. I finished the apple by the time she left.

"I met a couple in Red Ford last night who know your wife," I told him. "Milo Perkins and Gertrude."

"Oh?" He got a pleased smile. "Nice folks."

"They said to say hello to her if I had the chance."

He asked how they were doing and pretty soon suggested I go with him when he had lunch at noon. Biddy would like to hear what was going on since Aaron Feist was killed.

Another customer showed up, so I promised to come back before twelve, then took a walk up and down the main drag. About the only action I saw was when sparrows went at my Model T's grille, picking off squashed grasshoppers.

The junior Swenson's house was white with an open porch across the front. Two beat-up wicker chairs sat before the window facing the street. Evidently Pete had warned his wife by telephone that he was bringing a guest, because she welcomed me without surprise and had set the kitchen table for three.

Biddy was brown-haired, blue-eyed, and slim as a boy. Her smile seldom left, because her teeth were more than her lips could cover without an effort, and she wasn't a woman who'd strain.

During our lunch of ham sandwiches, I filled them in on the Aaron Feist murder. They listened all bug-eyed and solemn as Biddy's face would allow.

"Milo's right," Biddy said. "I always suspected Foxy was up to something sneaky when he fired Gertrude. I can tell you the haberdashery was taking in more money every month I was there. If Aaron's share wasn't going up, he was being cheated."

"Well," said Pete, "Aaron sure didn't do anything to help their sales, so I'd think Mr. Fox deserved to make more."

Biddy got her lips together in deep disapproval. "You think that gave him the right to kill Aaron, maybe?"

They went at it strong for a while—it was plain they'd argued before. I let it ride till they both ran down and finally asked Biddy if she thought anything suspicious went on between Stella and Fox.

"He'd have liked to get close to her, I'm sure of that. Whenever she'd come around he'd ask for her opinion of things like the window display and the way clothes were laid out on the counters. He always acted like whatever she said was just too, too smart. He'd tell her how she should be in the clothing business."

"What was he like—steady or moody?"

"Oh, he was a moody one. One day up and the next down. Nice as pie or mean as a tick. I went to work every day worrying about what he was going to be like."

"You never told me that," said her husband, scowling.

"Well, what use would it have been? You'd just say he had lots to worry about and I shouldn't take notice."

"Was he messing with any other women?" I asked.

"Well, he made and got some phone calls now and again. I passed on a couple from this woman with kind of a mannish voice."

"Never gave her name?"

"Oh, no. She talked kind of funny, like she might be trying to sound southern or something. It wasn't natural."

"You sure it wasn't Stella?"

The idea seemed to startle her. She thought a second before answering slowly, "No. I don't think so."

"How'd he act after one of these calls—up or down?"

"Mostly I'd say they gave him a lift. Once it was different, he got really owly."

I asked if she'd ever gone to dances where Aaron's band played, and she said of course. She'd met Pete when she came with some friends to Clifton for the dance.

"My friend Josie was crazy about the trumpet man, Doug Daley, and she talked three of us girls into coming over. Pete asked me for the first dance before I even sat down."

That surprised me some, because he didn't seem much of the go-getter. Eventually I found he'd had his first couple drinks earlier that night and was feeling frisky. When he saw her he told his friend she was the one for him. His friend bet him a pint he didn't have nerve enough to walk up and ask her right off for a dance. He took the bet.

"It was lucky I went with just girls," said Biddy. "If I'd come with a guy I'd have had to say no, and he'd probably never tried again."

She gave him a warmer smile, and he suddenly grinned back, losing all his sullenness. It made him seem young and vulnerable.

"You notice what Aaron did during intermission?" I asked.

"That's funny. I did. He went down off the bandstand and talked with this fat girl who was sitting close to the band. Pete told me she was Mary Ann Copeland—a wallflower crazy about musicians—who always comes to the dance early. Anyway, he was still with her when I got back from going out with Pete, only by then they were both drinking Cokes. Mary Ann was just glowing, she was so happy. It made me feel good for her. In case you're wondering, Pete and I just took a walk up and down Main Street—we weren't necking in a car. I wouldn't do that the first time I met a fella."

"You notice if Aaron talked to her after the dance?"

"No, I was paying all my attention to Pete by then, but I know the band always takes things down, packs up, and takes off like they were afraid their car'd turn into a pumpkin if they didn't scat like cats the second they finished 'Good-Night Ladies.' "

By this time I had finished the brownie she served for dessert and could see Pete was ready to head back for the store, so I thanked her and got up. At the door I asked where I'd find Mary Ann Copeland.

"She'd be at Bockoven's bakery. That's across the street from our store."

As we walked back to Main Street Pete told me he'd telephoned his pa, and the old man said the sign was okay as was. I wasn't all broken up, since I didn't care to hang around town that long anyway.

Mary Ann didn't look more than a pound or two past pleasingly plump to me, but it was normal for a woman slim as Biddy to call her fat. Small eyes and a button nose gave Mary Ann a moon face with a warm, clean smile.

She said hi and asked if she could help me.

"You might if you're Mary Ann Copeland."

"That's me."

"I hear you like dance bands."

The smile faded and she looked puzzled.

"I've just had lunch with the Swensons, Pete and Biddy," I said. "We were talking about the time Biddy first met Pete at a dance here in town. Biddy said you seemed to be pretty good friends with the leader, Aaron Feist."

Her face clouded up and she shook her head. "It's an awful thing," she said. "The murder."

"Awful," I agreed. Then I told her I was trying to learn as much as I could about Aaron to find out why he was killed.

"Everybody thinks they know why," she said, frowning at me.

"You think he was cheating on his wife?"

"No."

"Some think he was. Tell me why you think different."

"He wasn't a woman chaser, that's why. He was a dear sweet man—"

"What'd he talk to you about during intermission that time Biddy noticed you two together?"

"Mostly about bands and favorite songs. Then movies and what I liked in school."

"Did he ask you to take a walk or anything?"

"Not the first time he talked to me. But maybe three or four months later he took me over to Andy's Cafe and bought me a chocolate milk shake. He never tried to get me alone or make any passes."

"You wish he had?"

She looked past me a moment, smiled a little sadly, and said yes, she guessed she did. But she had never even dreamed he would.

I wasn't sure which of us she was trying to kid. We talked a little more, and when a customer came in I waved good-bye and left.

$\triangledown$

17

At Annabelle's house Hank, Kip, and Lenny were sitting in the backyard taking a break from wrestling practice.

"We found out something while you were gone," Hank told me.

"Like what?" I said, sitting down beside him.

"The guy that slugged Kip was Toughy O'Keefe. He lives on the north side and goes to parochial school."

"How'd you find out?"

He grinned. "Before lunch we took a bike ride over to the park. Along the way Kip recognized one of the gang that stopped him, so we sort of surrounded him and asked questions. We know where Toughy lives and that he's got four brothers, including a guy I know. Duke. I figure we can set up a rematch."

I glanced at Kip. He was trying to show interest but his eyes had a hunted look.

"You and this Duke friends?" I asked Hank.

"We've always got along."

That told me neither of them had ever been sure he could whip the other and they'd never got mad enough over anything to test it.

"How big are the brothers?"

"One's bigger than Duke, but slow. Two are sort of between Toughy and Duke."

So the odds'd be five against four at best. And I suspected the Irishmen had lots of friends.

"You set up this rematch, I want to know the details," I said.

"Oh, I figured you'd want in on it. And I'm pretty sure of Duke. It won't be a gang fight. Duke's fair."

"I don't trust fair in family fights. Keep me up on this. And meanwhile, keep practicing the throws," I told Kip. He nodded without enthusiasm. Lenny looked sympathetic.

While we were talking I saw Stella weeding in her garden. When our conference broke up I wandered over to the edge of her lot and said hi. She gave me a look that if I didn't know better I'd have thought was hot.

"Where've you been?" she asked.

"Over to Clifton."

She sat back on her heels, squinting a little against the sun. "Why there?"

"Wanted to talk with Biddy Swenson."

"Biddy—oh, yes, she worked at the store until she got married. Why?"

"Milo Perkins suggested it."

I got the feeling she wasn't as pleased with my work as she might be. She pulled off her cotton gloves and frowned.

"You seem to have been talking with all the old employees. Whatever for?"

"Learning a little about Gene Fox."

"Oh." Her "oh" was very small.

"What do you think of him?"

"He's very bright and capable—"

"He ever try moving in on you?"

"Whatever gave you that idea?"

"Biddy. She said he flattered you, asked your opinions. Stuff like that."

"What'd she say my reaction was?"

"She never said. Just told me he went out of his way to flatter your opinions and encourage your visits to the store."

She rose from the mat she'd been kneeling on, dusted her skirt with the loose gloves, and straightened her shoulders.

"Gene's been a perfect gentleman to me—there's nothing insincere about his appreciation for my suggestions about improving the window displays. Like most people around here, Biddy's prejudiced against anybody from east of the Mississippi. So's Milo. Just because Gene's smarter than they are and didn't grow up here, they despise him."

"It seemed to me they were more interested in your not taking the rap for Aaron's murder than in picking on a foreigner."

Right away she became apologetic. "I'm sure they mean well toward me. I'll admit all those people have been nice to me, but I just know they resented old Mr. Feist for bringing in Gene. I suppose it's natural."

"Okay. You don't believe Fox killed Aaron. I get the picture."

She turned aggressive. "It's a ridiculous notion. He's not the sort who'd stab anybody, not even in self-defense. How could anyone believe he would?"

"Cops generally believe what's easy because most of the time they'll be right. Okay. Maybe you're right about Fox. But it bothered me when I asked if he was alone Sunday night and he couldn't look me in the eye when he said yeah."

She said "oh" very casually.

"Was he visiting you or did you go to his place?"

She met me eye to eye and said neither.

"Has it ever happened?"

"No."

Nine times out of ten women are better actors than men, and I figured Stella was acting. It made me wonder if she'd been acting the night I was in bed with her, but I couldn't buy that. I've heard of women faking orgasms; hiding one seemed unlikely. On the other hand, I hadn't been with any other women accused of murder that I could remember.

"It'd be quite an alibi," I said.

"I don't need an alibi. I didn't kill Aaron."

"And you'd rather die than admit you were messing with Gene Fox, right?"

"I can't admit something I haven't done. I appreciate what you think you're trying to do for me, but the fact I let you into my bed doesn't mean I've slept with every man in town

or that I'll embarrass a man who's been a perfect gentleman
to me."

"The hitch is, cops'll figure if you two were together it was
done by the pair of you. You getting rid of a husband you
didn't want, him dumping a partner he didn't need."

She sagged a little, then straightened up and glared at me.

"Do you hate me because I didn't act like an animal with
you—?" She broke off as she stared over my shoulder, then
said, "There's someone to see you," and walked swiftly
toward the house.

I turned around and watched a stocky character in a shiny
blue suit strolling my way. From his grin I could tell he'd be
the friendly half of an interrogation team in the basement
at City Hall.

"Sergeant Rush," he told me. "Red Ford police. I been
hearing some about you, Wilcox."

"Probably all lies."

He chuckled. "Since we seem to be talking to the same
people, I figure we might as well compare notes some.
Okay?"

"Sure."

"I like to get to the gut right off. Who you figure for it?"

"Not sure."

"So who've we got? The wife, the partner, the neighbor
pair, maybe one of the boys from the band—like Frenchy."

"All possible," I granted. "I just can't quite figure any of
them for it."

"How about a passing tramp? No, I see you don't like
that. How'd he get hold of Stella's butcher knife, right? But
how'd anybody get hold of that except the lady you were
just talking to?"

"Anybody who'd been in the house. And they've all been
there, haven't they?"

He nodded cheerfully. "All in the last couple months. Old
Aaron brought everybody home. Except the neighbor lady
and her simple daughter. Somehow they never made it.
Maybe Stella didn't figure the girl was housebroke."

"That's not what you think."

"You're right. I think she was jealous. You know something I never can figure? Why women who can't stand their husbands get crazy jealous. You figure that?"

"Pride, I guess."

"Uh-huh. Likely. Lot of murders come that way. Only, Milo types usually don't kill. They get even different ways. Milo's got a hard-on for Gene Fox because he canned his wife and didn't appreciate his old salesman. He wouldn't stab anybody, right? But he'd sure love to get Fox in the soup."

"What'd he say to you?"

"Just about nothing. Doesn't want to be a witness, you know. So why'd he come on to you last night in Jacob's place?"

"You keep things covered," I said.

"That's the heart of my business, friend. Where'd you go this morning?"

"You don't know?"

"Went west, that's all. Figure probably Clifton. Where Biddy went after she married the Swede. She tell you anything?"

"She doesn't think Stella did it."

"Who'd she pick—Fox?"

"I got the notion she'd like it to be him."

"So Milo figured she'd put the finger on him and you'd figure out a way to nail him. What were you and Stella chinning about when I came around?"

"The same guy."

"She think he did it?"

"No. Says he's not the type."

"Maybe not. But look at his motives. The dead man's share and the wife. The whole pot, you might say."

"You got something says they've been cozy?"

"Just a hunch," he said with more innocence than I was able to believe in.

"Did you talk with Frenchy?" I asked him.

He nodded.

"What about his motive?"

"Not bad. He tries to make folks think he figured Aaron for some kind of saint, but he hadn't always put it that way to the boys in the band. He tried to make them think they were getting screwed on the percentages, and he reminded them regular they had a leader that couldn't read music. That seemed to make him pretty sore."

"He told me he'd been thinking about a band of his own but didn't move because he couldn't get enough good players."

"Yeah, there was that. But he had another little problem—dealing with dance hall owners. Most of them in our territory liked Aaron. They wouldn't have liked one of Aaron's boys breaking up the old outfit and competing for his dates."

"It doesn't seem like a big enough deal to kill for."

"Not for you or me. But I've known guys'd kill for a dime. You get a man like Frenchy, who figures he can be somebody big, they won't let anything stop 'em."

"Where was he Sunday night?"

"Home with his wife—if you can believe her."

"Do you?"

"I guess I'll have to unless I can prove her a liar."

Which told me he still liked Stella for the murder.

$\triangledown$

18

BEFORE HE LEFT I asked Sergeant Rush if he'd questioned Carrie about the murder. He said yeah, he and his partner asked questions, but the answers were all the same. The girl smiled sweetly, shook her head, and said, "Ask Mama."

"You wonder about her?"

"Elroy, my partner, figures it's an act. That she's nowhere near as dumb as her ma claims. I'm not so sure. I talked with her teachers at school, where she went before they gave up on her. They say she's like a bright and eager seven-year-old. Knows what's going on, but hasn't got any real hold of it all, you know?"

I poked around for his ideas about Fox; he said the guy was damned well named, and he was convinced if this bird killed anybody, he'd have a gold-plated alibi all ready and framed. That's why it had puzzled him some that the guy seemed to be hiding something about the night of the killing.

"He strikes me as cool enough to piss ice water, and the last guy around to go nuts and stab somebody like a maniac the way Aaron was done."

"So what if he figured things that way and deliberately made it look like a jealous woman did it?"

"Nah. I can't picture it. Guys like him want everything neat and squared away. If it came down to it, he'd more than likely fix up some kind of accident, or hire some hood to do the job. He comes from Chicago, you know. That's how they do things there."

"But you admit you think he's covering up something about what he was doing that night."

"Well, most of us got things to hide, right?" He grinned big. "What it comes down to, Wilcox, is your girlfriend, Darlene. It looks like you're gonna have to frame somebody else if you're gonna save her neck."

He left me with that, and after another cigarette I walked over to Darlene's. She answered the door as if she'd been standing there waiting for me. Her green and white house-dress gave her a fresh look and her hair was pinned up in a large bun. It made her hazel eyes wider and showed off her smooth neck. She smiled and tilted her head.

"Been watching out your window?" I asked.

The smile broadened.

"I was. Recognized the man questioning you. It was Sergeant Rush, wasn't it?"

"Yeah. Can we talk some?"

"Of course. I'll make coffee."

I followed her into a high-ceilinged kitchen lined with tall cabinets that had probably been cream-colored once, but time had turned them yellow. All the surfaces were clear and clean, the sink shiny.

I asked where Carrie was as Darlene filled a percolator at the sink.

"Off on a picnic with Norma Jans's folks. Norma's a lot like Carrie, and I'm good friends with her parents. I can trust them with her."

"Does Carrie help you cook when she's home?"

"You better believe it. I let her cut vegetables, peel potatoes, and prepare fruit, but she's afraid of fire and doesn't want to get near the stove."

She measured coffee into the percolator basket, put on the glass cover, and lit the gas burner with a wooden match.

We watched in silence as the water in the percolator began to bubble and burp up. Suddenly she glanced at me.

"What'd the sergeant ask you?"

"He heard I'd been snooping around, wanted to compare

notes, see if I'd uncovered anything. He's had me watched pretty good."

"And had you uncovered anything he wasn't aware of?"

"Nope. He tries to come on simple, but he isn't. On the other hand, he's not quite as smart as he likes to think he is."

She watched the water turn dark as it splashed against the glass percolator top.

"What'd he say about me?"

"He tried to make me think you were a prime suspect. I don't know if that was just to keep me in my place or if he thought maybe it'd goose me into working harder on this case."

"What'd he say about Carrie?"

"He thinks she's a nice, innocent girl."

She smiled warmly. "Well, that's good to hear."

"His partner, Elroy, isn't so sure."

The smile faded into a worried frown.

"He thinks Carrie's pretty, too, but Rush says he suspects she's more savvy than she lets on. I suppose that's natural. You see a girl who looks as great as she does, it's hard to believe that anything could be missing."

"I didn't like him—he has a mean face and a nasty voice and a mind to match."

"You mean Elroy, the sergeant's partner?"

"Yes."

"I haven't met him, but suppose I'm bound to. You said you and Carrie were in her room when all the fracas went on—that you went there when you had trouble sleeping. Was there something special worrying you that night?"

She glanced at the wall clock, then back to the percolator.

"I told you, I guessed that Carrie was expecting Aaron to come around. Of course I was worried—isn't that perfectly natural?"

"Sure. So you were in her room, reading to her with the door locked, and somebody followed him in and caught him on the stairs. Who else would know he was coming?"

"Isn't that perfectly obvious? His wife, of course. She no

doubt saw him cross the yard—her room looks this way. She certainly had reason to be suspicious of his interest in Carrie. He hadn't made any secret of it."

"When did you talk with Aaron last?"

"That afternoon he came around. He said he'd had an argument with Frenchy about the percentage they got. Frenchy claimed his count of the people there told him they got shortchanged by the dance hall owner, and there was talk of that all the way home. Arguments of any kind upset Aaron terribly. He admitted to me he knew the owner let personal friends in free, but he didn't think there were enough free passes to make that much difference. Aaron never could stand making a fuss. I'm afraid Frenchy was probably right about them being cheated."

"You think Frenchy'd get mad enough to kill Aaron?"

"Well, all I know about him is what Aaron told me. Aaron said he was terribly emotional, but gave me no reason to think he was some kind of maniac. On the other hand, Aaron wasn't the kind of man who'd be sensitive to something like that. I mean, he was so unemotional himself."

"So Aaron wasn't afraid of Frenchy?"

"Not physically. He just hated the sort of fuss that Frenchy was always causing."

We saw a brilliant flash of light through the kitchen windows, and as the thunder boomed I realized it had turned dark out. We got up and went to the window. Overhead the clouds were thick and rolling. As we watched, lightning flashed, thick, jagged, and blinding. We blinked as the thunder crashed again. She screamed and grabbed me as the house shook. Hell, I thought the whole earth trembled.

I put my arms around her when another flash of lightning followed by instant thunder made her moan in terror and clutch me tighter than ever.

"It's okay," I assured her, "we been missed twice already."

The next flash and thunderclap had a second's pause between them, and I told her that did it, three straight misses made it a sure thing we were safe.

She worked out of my bear hug but held on to my hand as she led me into the living room where, typically, the blinds had been drawn against the hot afternoon sun. We sat on the couch.

"I'm sorry I got hysterical," she whispered. "Thunderstorms terrify me—my father was killed by lightning when I was only five. He was standing in front of the barn door, watching the approaching storm—"

Another thunderclap made her jump, and I put my arm around her. She felt soft and warm even with her arms tense.

The rain came in a rush, spattering against the windows and drumming on the roof. Then there was hammering hail.

Darlene pushed her head against my chest and hung on like a child.

In a few minutes it was all over, and the sun came out. Slowly she recovered, raised her head, and straightened up. She looked around in a daze, then turned to face me. Our heads weren't a foot apart.

"Well," she said, "our coffee'll be ruined."

She started up, but when I pulled her back she collapsed gently onto my lap, murmured something too soft to hear, and opened her mouth when I kissed her.

Her hands clutched the back of my head, pressing me closer. When we moved beyond the kissing, she was quick and eager to help. In fact she got so helpful we nearly fell off the couch, and I scrambled like a drunk monkey for several seconds trying to avoid a broken tail. She whispered, don't hurry, but wasn't a damned bit helpful in slowing things down. I didn't have a prayer of making it last and heard her moan "No" when she sensed it. I told her to hang on, there'd be more.

There was.

I've been lucky with quite a few women—enjoyed a good many younger, maybe prettier, and even spryer loving ones—but Darlene was an artist at experiencing complete satisfaction and letting me know all about it.

Afterward, while we rested, she kept murmuring, "Lovely, lovely. Oh, that was so lovely!"

And then she slipped away, kissed me, gathered her clothes, and went upstairs.

She came back wearing a light housecoat and had let her hair down. I got another hot kiss before she went to make fresh coffee.

We drank it while she talked about her mother marrying another farmer who went broke, so they moved to Webster, where Darlene became a servant for an old attorney who married her two years before he died.

"You said you were 'a widow of a kind' when we first talked. Why'd you say it that way?"

She laughed.

"It made you awfully curious, didn't it?"

"Yeah. I figured you were divorced or something."

"Or maybe not even been married?"

"Well, I thought of that."

"So I didn't want to seem like just another woman who outlived her husband. Only, it's hard to play the gay divorcée when you've got a daughter who's simple and so pretty she gets all of the attention."

We talked some more, then she said she'd ask me to supper but Carrie'd be home soon and she wasn't comfortable with guests at meals.

I didn't believe that, but said good-bye and went out, wondering a little at her not wanting a farewell kiss after she'd turned so romantic so sudden.

With women, there's no way to figure.

∇

19

"I WANT YOU to be particularly careful what you say at supper tonight," Annabelle told me as I joined her and the two boys in her kitchen. "We're having company."

"Who?"

"Well, I thought it'd be nice to have Stella over since she's still upset about being a widow, and since she's going to be a real partner in business with Gene, I asked him to join us."

"You mean Gene Fox?"

"Who else?"

"Boy, Annabelle, you're subtle as an Irish bouquet. Aaron's not cool in his coffin and you're already making like cupid for Stella?"

"What's an Irish bouquet?" asked Kip.

"A brick," Hank told him.

"This has nothing to do with romance," Annabelle informed me. "It's business, and business can't wait. Now, when we're eating, don't say anything about the murder or the trial, okay?"

"What do you figure this crowd's gonna talk about, the weather?"

"If you don't bring up all the unpleasantness, they certainly won't, and I don't want you cross-examining my guests over fried chicken and mashed potatoes."

I promised to keep my yap shut through the meal but didn't promise anything about before or after, and she didn't think to warn me against that.

It was plain to me that Hank was excited over having

Stella to dinner, but hated having Fox come—his face was a study as he tried to balance the whole business. Kip, as usual, looked eager. He loved company, especially women, because they almost always made a big fuss over him.

Stella showed up first and joined Annabelle in the kitchen, where she didn't do anything helpful but talked a lot. She was all hopped up about a trip she was planning to Chicago, and rattled on about it. Annabelle got so interested that Stella started pushing for her to come along, saying they'd have a great time and she needed a vacation from homemaking.

Scott, the boys, and I were in the living room, where we could take it all in. I could see Scott getting more and more tense as Stella went on. Finally, he stood up and went into the kitchen and reminded them in a tone heavy with sarcasm that it wasn't likely Stella would be traveling far until after the trial.

That needle flattened the dialogue for a moment before Annabelle got her wind back, and let him know in the severest tones I ever heard her use on him that they were perfectly aware the trip couldn't start until matters were cleared up.

Her uncharacteristic sharpness threw Scott momentarily, but of course just got his mad into higher gear. He made it plain they were taking too much for granted about how available Stella might be for travel once the jury did its job.

Annabelle suggested he ought to be out in the living room when their other guest showed up, and he finally got smart and left them alone.

From then on, conversation in the kitchen was kept on a level too low for eavesdropping.

When Gene Fox finally arrived, Scott greeted him as if they were old war buddies, and Fox responded like a man who owned a clothing store and was in his favorite customer's house. I wasn't surprised they started talking clothes and took a while before I horned in. Since we weren't eating yet, I asked Fox what Sergeant Rush was after during his afternoon visit.

I don't think it had occurred to him before then that I was the bum who'd been in his store asking questions and buying a cheap pair of corduroys. He looked at me with some surprise before answering with careful casualness.

"It was nothing, really. He tried to make me say I was with someone Sunday night. Says if I can't prove I was home, it will make me a suspect in the murder."

He looked at Scott. "It's all crazy, you know. Why in the world would I kill him? Aaron and I had a complete understanding—killing him wouldn't gain me a nickel."

Scott glanced toward the kitchen, then leaned forward and in a stage whisper asked if he thought Stella had done it.

With too heavy assurance, Fox said, "No, of course not."

I horned in again. "He ask you any questions about whether Aaron had ever questioned the income figures you paid him his share from?"

"As a matter of fact, he did." Fox's smile was condescending. "Only someone completely ignorant of Aaron would ever think of such a question. When I was first running the store, I tried to talk to Aaron about profit margins and precisely how our shares would work out. He always just shook his head and waved me off. Things like that bored him stiff. He'd say, 'You handle all that, don't bother me with it. I don't want to know.' "

"Did he ask you how cozy you were with Stella?"

I got the condescending smile again.

"You people all think alike, don't you? Yes, of course. I could understand him asking that, but it surprises me you would. If she and I were lovers, she'd be at least an accomplice, wouldn't she?"

So he knew my role, that my assignment from Annabelle was to keep her friend Stella in the clear.

Annabelle appeared in the kitchen doorway, gave me a warning look, and said everyone should be ready to come to the table in two minutes.

Once at the table, Scott took over, starting with stories about life on the road and moving on to jokes. He knew dozens about traveling salesmen but did his specialties in Norwegian, Scottish, and Yiddish accents. After a while Annabelle felt Scott was hogging things and suggested Kip recite one of the historical parodies from the "Norse Nightingale." Kip turned bashful for a few seconds but pretty soon started in on "The Midnight Ride of Paul Revere," opening with "Listen Christina and you skal hear/ 'bout midnite ride of Paul Rawere. . . ."

It got good laughs and he only stumbled once, so of course he volunteered to do "Horatious at the Bridge," but his mother said he should save that for another time, then turned to ask Fox if he'd thought any of bringing Stella into the store's operation. He'd been totally silent through the meal, and was obviously grateful for a chance to take the stage.

"Funny you should ask. It's exactly what I've been thinking, but it seemed I ought to wait awhile. I know she's loaded with great merchandising ideas."

He beamed at her and she smiled back before turning thoughtful.

"I've some ideas we've never talked about."

"Wonderful. Tell me—I mean, us."

"I think we should put in a women's wear department. Would that upset you?"

He gave me a look I couldn't figure for sure, but it was almost proud. Then he smiled at her. "Not if you agreed to take charge of it. I simply wouldn't know where to start."

"I'm not at all certain I do either. Do you know someone in Chicago I could talk to if I went there for a visit?"

Fox absolutely glowed. "As a matter of fact, I do. There are two or three women I know that you could see. By golly, this is wonderful—you've been thinking about this, haven't you? These gals are just the ones who can tell you what's in style and where we could get decent prices and prompt delivery. We could start nice and easy, of course. See what sort of reaction we get from townsfolk."

All of this was exactly what Annabelle had been wanting to promote, but once it was so obviously working she began to worry about the way she'd put Scott down earlier and the way he was now reduced to sullen munching while guests dominated his table. She asked him what he thought of the chances for a women's department in the store, and he granted, a little grudgingly, that it might work out fine.

Fox caught on and helped push the dialogue Scott's way by asking him his impression of this year's farm crops as he traveled over the state. Scott said the only thing he saw really thriving was grasshoppers.

After finishing all the groceries in sight, the men left the cleanup to the women and went back in the living room where Scott and Fox started discussing politics. Kip disappeared upstairs, Hank drifted outside. I listened to the two guys, who agreed things might get better under Roosevelt eventually, but neither of them felt excited about prospects for the country in general, or North Dakota in particular. In the end they agreed everything was in God's hands, and even he seemed to have lost interest in us.

As I expected, Fox walked Stella to her door across the yard. I scooted up to Hank's room, which overlooked the Feist house, and looked down. The couple stood a few minutes at the back door before he shook hands with her and left. I guessed he was cute enough to figure I'd be watching and made a point of keeping the relationship looking innocent.

$\triangledown$

20

ALITTLE AFTER nine that evening I headed for the Eastside. There'd been Fourth of Julys when Corden turned pretty lively, but the Eastside on a Saturday night made my hometown look like a cemetery. Jacob's place was mobbed by men two and three deep at the bar, laughing and yelling like the booze was free. It was enough to give a man a buzz, just looking on.

I eased through the mob and was pulled up short on spotting Frenchy on a stool beside Doug Daley, the trumpet man.

"What happened to the dance you guys were supposed to be playing?" I asked, squeezing in between them.

"Crapped out," snarled Frenchy, glaring at me in the mirror. "Old Gus wouldn't play and that goddamn Ford agreed—said they hadda respect the dead. That figures, don't it? Since both of them're about as good as dead themselves. Far as I'm concerned, they're sure as hell dead with the band. I wouldn't use them sons of bitches even if they was good. Hell, old Doug here, and me, we're the only musicians in the lot."

"What about Max?"

"Oh, Max is okay. Just a kid, but he's coming."

I glanced at Doug, who showed no interest in Frenchy's flattery or complaints. He was staring at a booth, where two young women leaned across their table in eager talk.

Frenchy kept bitching. "Those bastards have got me in Dutch with the dance hall owner in Corden, and word'll get around, sure as hell."

Doug slipped off his stool and headed toward the booth with the two young women.

Frenchy glared at his back.

"Can't even depend on him," he told me. "He doesn't give a shit what happens if he can just get laid. That's got to be the horniest son of a bitch that ever blew a trumpet."

I thought of suggesting that Frenchy work himself into a one-man band so he'd be in complete control, but squelched the line and leaned close.

"He ever try moving in on Stella?"

"You kidding? He's tried every broad he's ever seen."

"Get anywhere?"

"Maybe third base. Back in the days when she rode with the band, you can bet on it he was feeling her up. After a while she wouldn't sit on his lap. She didn't make a big thing of it, didn't want to worry Aaron. As if anything really would. God, what a dimwit."

"She didn't complain, then?"

"Hell, I think she loved it, but she was afraid he'd get too big ideas, which of course he did. She's strictly a teaser. I bet not even Aaron's ever really got in there. Probably what made him such a nance."

"Seems more like it'd put him on the prowl."

"Most guys, it would. But old Aaron, he just shriveled up. Didn't hustle anybody but wallflowers and kids. He'd sit next to them all through intermission, being the sweet and lovable big brother. Safe, you know?"

It didn't figure. The whole business was beyond me. If all he was after was safe, how the hell did he wind up a bloody mess on his neighbor's stairway?

"Did Doug ever try for Aaron's neighbors, Darlene and daughter?"

"The simple kid? He would if he'd caught her alone, you can bet. Just his speed. That Darlene kept her strictly under cover. And since they never came to dances or hung around bars, Doug never got a shot at the mama. So far he's not got around working door to door, but it could come to that."

Poor Doug. He'd never know what he'd missed. On the other hand he probably wouldn't have appreciated her even if he'd made out. I liked to think he couldn't have gotten anyplace with her no matter what.

Frenchy got tiresome, and after wishing him a wild night I left. Doug was still making his pitch to the two young women, who kept looking at each other and laughing at him. It was plain he wasn't getting anywhere. Hustling two women at a time almost never works, especially if they're friends.

Sunday afternoon Hank went around and talked with Duke O'Keefe. They finally agreed to match up Kip and Toughy the following Saturday at Ford Park. Hank told me he wasn't letting Kip in on the plan until Saturday morning, and I agreed that was smart. Meanwhile we'd put him through the wrestling tricks so he'd have them down cold enough to do automatically.

Annabelle invited Stella to supper again Sunday night, but she seemed a little vacant through most of the meal. That worried Kip. About halfway through he asked Stella if she missed Mr. Fox. Of course that upset Annabelle, but it only made Stella laugh and tell him he was very sensitive and understanding.

She admitted she'd wanted to discuss starting a women's wear department in the store but had missed seeing Gene in his yard. She tried telephoning but he hadn't answered.

We learned Monday that while we discussed him Sunday evening, he was dead on his bed with his throat cut from ear to ear. A bloody boning knife lay on the floor under his dangling right hand beside the bed.

$\triangledown$

21

ALL MONDAY AFTERNOON and into the evening, Sergeant Rush and Elroy Burns questioned just about everybody in town who'd so much as bought a tie from Fox. It was well past supper when they started on me. Smoke was thicker than Bertha's split pea soup as we sat there squinting at each other in a stingy bare room over a scarred table.

Elroy's droopy jowls and sagging skin under the eyes gave him a mournful expression that didn't fit Darlene's description of him as the total son of a bitch, and I decided she was just sore because he'd crowded her precious daughter and probably been impatient.

Burns took me though all my Saturday night travels and on to when I hit the hay at Annabelle's around one A.M. No, I couldn't vouch for where Annabelle and Scott were, I hadn't checked on them when I got home, didn't look in Hank or Kip's rooms, and hadn't heard anybody come or go.

"What time you figure you passed out?" Elroy asked. The leer and nastiness of that abruptly changed my opinion of Darlene's judgment of the bastard.

"I went to sleep in about twenty seconds, as usual. If anybody came or went, I'd have heard because I sleep light."

"You check on the neighbors when you came home?"

"Both houses were dark. I didn't look Fox's way since I couldn't see his place from anywhere but the kitchen, and I didn't go out there."

"What'd you people talk about at supper Saturday night?"

asked Rush. His approach was all friendly curiosity—no
accusation.

I told him about Stella's idea of starting a women's wear
department at the store, and her plans about making a trip
to Chicago to talk with people Fox referred her to.

"You and Fox talked about what the sergeant asked him,"
accused Elroy.

"Why not?"

Elroy sneered. "What'd he tell you I said?"

"He said you told him he needed an alibi real bad. Is that
right?"

Rush grinned, Elroy scowled.

"It's a fact."

"Yeah, but he got the notion you thought he'd be smart
if he made one up."

He waved that off and leaned over the table, giving me a
nasty grin. "What'd you say if I was to tell you we got a
witness saw Stella going into Fox's house the night of the
first murder?"

"I'd say either your witness is lying or Stella and Fox got
an alibi for that night. How'd your witness know Stella in
the dark?"

"People recognize lots of things about each other without
they have to see them face-to-face in daylight. Way they
walk, how they dress, their moves . . ."

"Yeah, sure. They get especially good at it when the guy
asking questions also offers the answers. I've been through
that routine—hell, I've used it. So what do you figure—the
two of them killed Aaron and then she killed Fox so he
couldn't rat on her?"

"You got anything better?"

"I don't see Stella butchering Aaron the way it was done.
They'd fought before, but she never hit him with anything
but her hands and she didn't give a damn about him, so I
don't see her going nuts about him getting cozy with a kid
like Carrie, especially if Stella was fooling around like you
claim."

Elroy settled back, watching me with his mean eyes. "The way I see it, Stella had been getting screwed by Fox, got enough, started home, spotted hubby going into Singer's place, ran into her kitchen, grabbed her knife, caught him on the stairs, and let him have it. Then she lost her head and dropped the knife when she ran back home. From the timing, old Fox probably guessed what'd happened and kept quiet, because he could see if she beat the rap he'd have her over a barrel and could wind up owning the store clear. After the sarge let him know he could get tabbed for it, he more'n likely told Stella, sorry, sweetheart, I think you better cop a plea, and she said fine, took him to bed, and when he was nice and wore out, slit his gullet."

"Neat," I said. "I can just picture Stella tearing into her house, digging up the butcher knife, running across the yard, through the back door, on through the kitchen and hallway, and up the stairs where she caught poor old Aaron, who'd only managed to reach the landing in all that time, and even when he heard her running up behind him, he just let her stab him out of sheer politeness."

"Okay," said Sergeant Rush. "Give us something better."

"I can't match your partner's wild imagination. What are the other possibilities? Maybe the woman screwing Fox that night was Frenchy's wife. What do you know about her?"

"We know she says she was alone both murder nights."

"She's alone most nights. So no alibi, just like Stella."

"And no motive."

"You don't know. Did you get to question Carrie?"

They nodded.

"Alone?"

"Tried it," said Elroy. "She clammed up. Wouldn't talk without Mama right beside. And when Mama was beside, all she'd do was back up anything she said. Since they were together all the time the murder was being committed on the steps, that seems solid."

"You show Carrie the knife?"

"Why would we do that?" demanded Elroy.

"I know," said Rush. "To see if she recognized it and if it'd been around the house before. That what you're thinking?"

I nodded. "Aaron did all kinds of chores around their place. Maybe one of them called for heavy cutting and he took the butcher knife over, then left it because Stella never used it."

"Whatever," said Rush, turning to Elroy. "Get the knife, we'll go talk with Carrie again."

Rush turned me down when I offered to go along. They gave me a ride back to Annabelle's, then went to Darlene's door. I smoked and watched from the front porch swing. When they came out sometime later I was waiting by their car.

"What'd she say?" I asked.

Rush shook his head. "Never saw it."

"You believe her?"

"Hard not to. She's a good kid."

Elroy didn't look impressed but kept his sad mouth shut and started the engine.

"Did you find prints on the knife near Fox?" I asked Sergeant Rush.

"Whose do you guess?"

"Fox's."

"Okay. Even so, somebody could've wrapped his fingers around the handle after the cutting."

"Did they?"

"We'll see."

I looked past him at Elroy, who scowled, shoved the gearshift into low, and started off.

▽

22

THERE WAS A light in Darlene's kitchen when I wandered around back. I saw her pass the window a couple times and decided Carrie was already up in her room.

Darlene answered my knock, looking fearful as she tried to peer through the screen.

"Carl?" she whispered.

"Yeah. Let me in."

She pushed the screen open and lifted her face as we paused in the vestibule. I kissed her. She pressed hard against me and brought both arms around my neck.

"Be very quiet," she whispered. "Carrie's up in her room but probably isn't asleep yet. She's very upset with all the excitement and those policemen. Wait here while I turn off the kitchen light."

A second later she returned, took my hand, and led me through the kitchen and dining room into her parlor.

"I'm so glad you've come—I was sure you would. I've been terrified."

"Why, what's scaring you?"

"Stella's mad. She's got to be. Who else'd kill Aaron and Gene? And she's probably been told by the police that I said she must have been the one who did it, and I'll be next. I'm so afraid—hold me!"

It got beyond holding in short order and turned frantic. She told me to hold my hand over her mouth, which took some doing with all the other action involved but didn't distract me enough to spoil the game by more than a fraction.

It all seemed to have a soothing effect on her fears. After the first round she was so sleepy any entertainment I wanted I had to take on my own. Attempts to bring her around enough to answer questions went nowhere.

Finally I whispered in her ear.

"I think I should go up and talk with Carrie."

Her body stiffened under me.

"What about?"

"What Aaron said about why he had to visit her that night in her room."

"It wouldn't do any good now. She'd be too sleepy to make any sense."

"Does she really know what happened?"

"I'm not sure. You can never tell about her. She keeps thinking Aaron will be around again. She won't believe he can't come."

"She ever been interested in any other men?"

"Only to the extent of wanting their approval. She has a great need that way. It isn't at all sexual. Can we make love again?"

That question sidetracked my detecting talents and sounded like a challenge, which, with her considerable cooperation, I managed to meet in what I considered grand style. It took a while but neither of us minded, and for quite a spell no other questions came to mind. Later it occurred to me that was her whole idea, but somehow that didn't spoil anything.

I never had a fight in my life that took more starch out of me than Darlene's loving.

▽

23

Scott kissed Annabelle good-bye at half past eight Monday morning and set off on his weekly crusade to sell every store owner in his territory a brand-new cash register. As far as I could tell, he never worried about Annabelle or his family while he was away, and Annabelle was absolutely confident in his ability to take care of himself. There were no telephone calls between them while he worked on the road. They shared a kind of childish faith that nothing could go wrong while they were apart two thirds of each year. I guess not having any imagination saves most folks from going nuts worrying.

A little before ten Tuesday I ambled over to Al Hamilton's office downtown. The dragon was outraged by my showing up without an appointment, but while she was letting me know that, Al came to his office door, told her it was okay, and waved me in.

I gave him the rundown on my activities the past week, and he made notes on a yellow legal pad with a fat red fountain pen while every so often looking up to scowl at me.

"You really getting anything from all this?" I asked finally.

"Not even writer's cramp," he sighed, sitting back. "It amounts to zero."

"So why write it down?"

"Habit. Started it when I was first admitted to the bar. Found it impressed the clients. They figured I was taking everything they offered seriously."

"Why don't you have your dragon take it down?"

"She'd actually do it, and I don't need all that crap. This Elroy who works with Rush, you think he's smart?"

"He generally knows his business. Rush's no fool either. They've got nothing really solid going but Stella, so they're stuck with her. They can't just say they've got no idea who did it."

"Naturally. That's the greatest weakness of our whole legal system—the fact you've always got to have a guilty party and sometimes nobody at hand is."

"My problem is, how do I get to talk with Carrie alone? She can be the key to this whole damned mess, but you can't get her away from Darlene long enough to open her up."

He nodded, then frowned. "Doesn't she leave Carrie with the Jans family now and again?"

"Yeah."

"All right. They're cousins of mine. I'll see what we can arrange."

I walked over to the bank after leaving the attorney and asked to talk with the head man. The cashier I spoke to looked a little uncomfortable about it, but went through a door in back and after a few moments came out followed by a squat gent in a black suit, white shirt, and dark tie. Looked all set for a funeral. He came to the little gate they had separating the sheep from the goats and said yes? in a tone that was strictly negative.

I told him not to worry, I wasn't looking for a loan or even a handout—just a little information. It was nice to see my approach didn't strike him as offensive; he actually grinned and asked for my name. As it registered, his grin broadened. He pushed the gate open, tipped his head toward the door behind him, and we went inside.

"So what information are you after?" he asked after he'd taken his seat behind his big desk and planted me in a padded chair facing him.

"You know why I'm in town?" I asked.

"I've heard rumors but am not sure of the facts. I take it

you're Annabelle's brother, the itinerant sleuth from South Dakota?"

"Bull's-eye."

"And you're supposed to help her friend, Stella?"

"You don't miss a beat."

"So what do you want from me?"

"You have a lady named Gertrude working here. A few years back she did the books for Feist's Haberdashery. She was let go there and came to work at this bank. It seems Gene Fox didn't think she was a good bookkeeper. Since she's been with you people awhile, you must think different, or does she have a job that isn't very special?"

"On the contrary, Gertrude is highly competent. In addition she gets on well with other employees and the general public, although she doesn't meet many of our customers directly."

"Since you know about everything in town, would you have any notion why Gene let her go?"

His smiled faded only slightly.

"I suspect at least two things could have been involved. First, Gertrude is not all that attractive physically. But perhaps more important, she is extremely meticulous, and I suspect Gene Fox, God rest his soul, was not too anxious to have such a careful and thorough party keeping records that were the basis for the division of income at the store."

"You know anything about Gertrude's husband?"

"Milo Perkins? Not much. He's never borrowed money or established a savings account. I recall hearing some talk by folks who knew the couple and were surprised when Milo kept working for Fox after Gertrude was fired. Some presumed he couldn't afford to quit, which was probably true, and everyone took it for granted he was kept on because Fox didn't want folks to think he was getting rid of people whose only mistake was still thinking of the store as a Feist operation. Firing them both would have offended the locals."

"Maybe he stayed on to see if he could expose Fox's cheating of Aaron."

"From what I've heard of Milo, that's quite likely. He's not the sort of man to forgive a wrong against his wife. If he'd been the one fired, he would have accepted that easily, but he's extremely protective and proud of Gertrude. I'm not quite sure why, since she's never struck me as a terribly vulnerable woman."

I thanked him and left the bank.

▽

24

IT WAS STILL nearly an hour before lunchtime, so I went back to Annabelle's neighborhood and tapped on Stella's door. When there was no answer I knocked harder. After a while steps approached. There was a pause as she looked through the window at me for a moment. Slowly she opened the inner door.

"What do you want?" she asked, sullenly.

"Wondered what you were doing. You okay?"

"I look a fright," she said, touching her hair. "I couldn't sleep last night."

"Cops give you any trouble?"

"They gave me hell. Do you know they claim to have a witness who saw me go into his house a week ago?"

"Yeah, I heard."

"It's a lie. I never went there. Never. If someone says they saw me, they're lying, and I can guess who it was—that damned Darlene."

"Maybe we should talk in the house."

"No. That'd get reported, too."

I thought she was going to close the door, but instead she pushed the screen open and came out on the stoop.

"We'll talk in the garden," she said.

But at first we didn't. We just walked out there and stood awhile with her staring at her crop and me looking at her face. It looked older, which didn't make her any less attractive, and for the first time I felt sure she couldn't have killed Aaron.

"Look," I said, "I need more help if I'm going to do you any good. I told Sergeant Rush and his stooge I didn't believe their witness, okay? Now answer some questions for me."

"I answered all the questions I could stand yesterday."

"Okay, forget it. Maybe Al can make your case."

She folded her arms across her breasts, took a deep breath, and said, "Oh, hell, ask."

"Did Aaron ever tell you he thought Fox was shorting him on his share of the store's profits?"

She shook her head.

"Didn't you ever wonder?"

She looked at me. "What're you getting at?"

"One of the old employees, a bookkeeper, got fired not long after Fox took over. Seems he thought she wasn't doing the job right. That sounds funny considering she went to work for a bank right after. She's still with them—the bank president thinks she's great on all counts. Fox did his own bookkeeping after she left. Isn't that enough to make you wonder?"

She shrugged. "Gene was a fussy, precise man. He got all upset because she drew a line for cents instead of putting in the two zeros after the point. He said it was a sign of sloppy thinking."

"How'd he happen to tell you this?"

"He was defensive about firing Gertrude because she'd been with the store so long. The first time I was in after she left, I asked about her, and right away he told me all about his concerns with her. He assured me he'd given her a full two weeks' notice and a nice reference letter. I really think he felt guilty about firing her."

"He say anything to you when Biddy left the job?"

"No. She hadn't been there a long time like Gertrude and never worked for Aaron's father, so I never really knew her. Do you know why she left?"

"Nope. Never asked when we talked. Had the feeling she wouldn't tell me while her husband was around."

"Why?"

"Well, during their gab about Fox, Biddy got critical, and

the husband took Fox's side. He said if Fox cheated Aaron, it was okay because he did all the work. I got a feeling Biddy and her husband had scrapped about that before."

"You think he made a pass at her and she was afraid to tell her husband because she thought he'd accuse her of leading him on?"

"Uh-huh."

She smiled. "You understand women awfully well for a man of your type."

I thought it was more like I understood husbands of his type, but let it pass.

"Do you understand me well enough to know I didn't kill Aaron?"

"I like to think so. I don't think you cared enough about him to have done anything so messy."

She suddenly smiled the way she had before we shared her bed.

"Really? You believe that song that says we only hurt the ones we love? I think you're a romantic, Carl. Under that rough exterior there's a poet. Would you care to tell me about what Darlene said to you when you visited her? Like last night?"

The question startled me enough to make me try tilting her back on the defensive.

"She said she was afraid you'd try to kill her. Maybe it was only an act, but it was a good one. She really sounded like she believed it."

"And fell all over you as her savior. I'm sure it was convincing. No man would ever doubt such an appeal. But go on, what was your reaction?"

I was stuck for a moment. Couldn't remember saying anything, then recalled the clinch that followed, waved my hand casually, and lied. Said I told her she had nothing to worry about.

Stella thanked me with enough sarcasm to draw blood. I gave it up and went back to Annabelle's.

▽

25

Hᴀɴᴋ ᴍᴇᴛ ᴍᴇ at the back door of Annabelle's. He said we had a problem.

"Kip was at the store with Lenny a while ago. On the way back Toughy went by in a car with some older guys and yelled at him, saying he'd see him Saturday."

"Oh, great."

"He asked me was it set and I couldn't lie to him, could I?"

"No. What'd he say?"

"Just looked sick. Which is what he's gonna be. He did that once before when he was afraid of a guy in school back in the third grade. We couldn't figure out what was the matter. He just kept saying he was sick—he looked it—and wouldn't get out of bed. We didn't know what it was all about until a teacher called after he was out two days."

I went in the house, found the door of his room closed, and tapped on it. When he said yeah, I went in.

He was flat on the bed, belly down and face toward the wall. I parked on the bed's edge and said, "We won't let him kill you, you know."

No response.

"Look. Lots of guys fight lots of times and don't wind up looking like me. If you wrestle him like Hank and I taught you, he can't punch you out, okay?"

Slowly he rolled over on his back and stared at the ceiling.

"I get all weak. Won't be able to raise my arms."

"Go for him quick. Your legs'll work. Just throw yourself at his thighs, knock him down, surprise him. You get a guy confused enough, he's easy to handle. When he goes down, roll free and when he comes at you, duck, grab an arm, and heist him over. The minute the action starts, you'll be fine. You get too busy to be scared. Just keep your head down, watch his feet, and you can keep track of where he's going. Stay low, hunch your shoulders, keep your hands up and open. That'll throw him off. Guys like Toughy just burrow in, swinging wild. You stay low, he's got no target."

I got him off the bed and told him to come on swinging, I'd show him what to do. He started feebly while I squatted and covered, all the time telling him to come on, swing, keep swinging. His small fists pummeled my forearms, getting to my shoulder a couple times, but I made sure he never touched my head.

When he was puffing good I straightened up and said okay, you saw what I was doing, now you do it.

He didn't like it but finally went ahead. I cuffed him with open hands, always making sure I got his arm or elbow and once just grazed his head.

"Okay, now when I get in close, go down fast, grab my knee, and shove your shoulder into my gut."

He didn't do it too well, but I let him tumble me. The next minute his mother was in the room wanting to know what in the world I thought I was doing.

I said I was teaching him tumbling tricks. She told me roughhousing was for outside and in the future don't do it in the house. Meantime, come down and eat lunch.

After we got through eating, Lenny Krueger showed up, and Hank and I got them going through the wrestling drills again. Kip worked hard but wasn't sharp. When they were well tuckered out I took them to the neighborhood store, bought a round of ice-cream cones, and suggested they go play at Lenny's house. When they were gone I told Hank we ought to move up the match.

"If he's got nearly a week to worry about this scrap he won't be worth a damn."

He said he'd go see Duke.

I went out back and looked toward Darlene's house but
didn't see any action. After a stroll around the yard I went
over and tapped on her back door. It took about ten seconds
for her to answer. Then she opened the door, stepped back,
let me walk past her, shut it, and hooked my arm so we met
belly to belly. I traded kisses with her, tilting my head back.

Her eyes were sleepy. She smiled.

"I was hoping you'd come," she whispered.

I was tempted to say a kiss wouldn't do it but managed to
shift my thinking a tad north and worked free enough to take
her elbow and move her into the kitchen.

"Let's talk first," I said.

"We can do that in the bedroom. Carrie's at the Janses'."

"We wouldn't talk in the bedroom."

"Sure we will. I'll talk to you all the time you do it. I'll tell
you what a wonderful lover you are and what I want to do
for you, and you can tell me what you want most."

It didn't seem polite to tell a lady in that mood that I had
a different line of chatter in mind, and to tell the truth the
different line went out of my head completely until she'd
exhausted her subject, not to mention me.

When she was quiet and my brain slipped back into low
gear, I asked if she was the one who reported seeing Stella go
into Fox's house a week ago last night.

She stirred, pulled her face back a few inches, and looked
in my eyes.

"Why do you ask?"

"One of the cops told me they've got a witness who says
she did. You're a neighbor, you could have looked out."

"If I'd seen it happen, don't you think I'd have told you?"

"Maybe not. You know I'm trying to help her out. You
might figure I'd think you were trying to pin it on her because
you already suspect and are scared of her."

She rose on one elbow, pushed her pillow around, and
settled on her back with her hands clasped behind her head.

"Okay. You're very cagey. It's hard to accept the fact you
understand me so well I can't hide things from you. A

woman can't quite imagine a man able to do that. I didn't tell the police I saw Stella go into Gene's house the Sunday before last. I told them I'd seen her go in there other times, though, because I did. She was his mistress. I've been waiting to see if you'd figure that out for yourself. I didn't want to hit you over the head with it because I was afraid it'd make you sore at me."

"Why'd you think she killed him?"

"Because the police were closing in and she was afraid Gene would put all the blame for Aaron's death on her, so she had to shut him up."

"That'd also make her the only suspect as Fox's killer."

"So maybe she lost her head. If the police convinced her he'd agreed to testify against her, she might have killed him over his betrayal and not cared about anything but punishing him for it. You want to make love again?"

I was only a little surprised that I didn't, but instead of admitting it, I told her I had to handle a problem involving my nephew and got up. She watched me pull on my clothes, smiled, pulled her heels up along the sheet, raised her parted knees, and bumped her hips wickedly.

I threw the hips a salute and left.

26

ANNABELLE SAID AL Hamilton had called, so I gave him a buzz. His dragon muttered something unfriendly before passing me on.

"I can't talk sense into my cousin," he told me. "She says Carrie's her daughter's best friend, and she won't do anything that might get Darlene in any trouble. Like everybody else in town, she thinks Stella killed Aaron and it's silly to upset anybody trying to prove different."

"Okay. Know anybody that's got a mouth organ?"

That threw him for a moment, but when I explained that Carrie wanted to play one, he gave it some thought and finally said yes, he had another cousin who owned a couple.

"Okay, let's hope this cousin will be more helpful. What we want is the simplest kind. For a learner."

He promised to check it out.

I saw Hank before supper. He gave me a nod, which I assumed meant he'd talked with Duke and made a change in the fight time.

After eating, he said it was set for seven-thirty, at Red Ford Park, down by the river.

"Does Lenny know?"

"Yup. He'll be with us."

At seven-twenty I thumbed Kip outside and suggested we take a walk. His expression told me at once he knew what was up. Slowly he got out of the rocker and followed me. Hank and Lenny were waiting at the corner.

"Remember what I told you," I said. "Go low, hit him at the knees, okay?"

He nodded miserably. We started toward the park, walking along the quiet street four abreast with me on his right, Lenny on the left, Hank next to him. Kip stared at the sky, which was clear pale blue all the way, and his expression was like he didn't think he'd see it again.

The air was still, and crickets were already tuning up for the night's chorus. We sighted a robin on the berm ahead of us, tugging at an angleworm. A speckle-breasted baby robin on a low branch nearby fluttered its wings and squawked for a feeding.

Kip said he wished he was a bird.

Hank told him if he was a robin he'd be dead already because they never lived as much as thirteen years. It was plain Kip thought being dead would beat this assignment.

I started talking to him again. "Keep moving, crowd him, stay low, and grab his arm when he swings. You can do it, don't worry, you're quick."

All the talk did was make him pull his head in farther, like a turtle. I thought that might help and told him to keep it up, he had the right idea. Head down, shoulders up.

The O'Keefes were waiting at the river's edge, clear of the trees growing along the upper bank. The earth was covered with cracked clay from the spring floods, which hadn't been very high, but there was still an area more than big enough for our business. The footing would be poor, which might make it hard for Toughy to get good leverage in his punches, but it'd also make dodging a little trickier for Kip. As I'd expected, we were well outnumbered. Besides the four brothers, there must have been half a dozen or more cousins. I was glad to see most of them were no bigger than Kip.

Toughy stood front and center, grinning like a fox over a bleeding chicken. The grin was enough to make me fight, but it hit Kip, who slowed his pace.

When we were two yards away, Toughy laughed out loud. "Hey, yellow belly, your uncle drag you here?"

The smaller kids jeered in echo, and suddenly Kip was gone from my side, charging like a little bull.

He didn't go for the knees or keep his hands low and open, he went in swinging. Toughy's grin turned to a snarl as he sidestepped and smacked Kip's head with a vicious swing. I saw Toughy's mouth pop open and guessed he'd at least jammed a knuckle, but the blow sent Kip sprawling. He rolled, came up, and charged so fast Toughy slipped trying to get set and was barreled over. When they came up, Toughy smacked Kip with a left that caught the top of his head and sent him scrambling to his knees. He came up like a bounced ball with fists flailing wildly. One of three swings clipped Toughy's mouth, splitting his upper lip. They both kept their feet through the next exchange and traded pretty evenly for several seconds before Kip suddenly caught the tough guy's fist with both hands, swung around, and threw him over his back. He flew beautifully. Kip didn't hang on as I'd told him to, so the fall didn't do any heavy damage. Toughy rolled over, scrambled to his feet, and charged. He was off-balance and his first swing only grazed Kip's skull as Kip ducked under and rammed his shoulder into Toughy's gut, then tried to straighten up. The weight and momentum took them both to the ground, but Toughy hung on. They rolled awkwardly for several seconds before Kip jerked free and regained his feet.

Toughy was slow getting up and for the first time didn't charge. He waited, panting heavily. Kip just watched.

"Come on, yellow belly," panted Toughy.

Kip lowered his head and waited. His gang yelled at Toughy as he charged, swinging wildly. Kip ducked, slipped clear, and threw a haymaker that caught his enemy smack on the nose and sent blood flying.

Toughy's face was a bloody mess by then. While he didn't quit, he was so winded he kept staggering. When I moved in to stop it a few seconds later, only the little kids in the O'Keefe crowd objected, but they were shut up quickly by Duke.

Hank walked over to Duke. They shook hands.

"He's a real scrapper," said Hank, "but he lost the fight when he hurt his hand on Kip's skull with that first punch. He couldn't hit worth a lick after that."

"He should've been able to take him with one hand. There'll be another time."

"There hadn't better be when Kip's alone and Toughy's got a gang."

Hank said that with a smile. Duke glanced back at his bigger brother, who looked at me. I gave him my "come and get it, sucker" smile. Big brother figured the odds, decided he didn't like them, went over to Toughy, put his arm around his shoulder, and headed him for home.

Duke took all that in, nodded politely at me, and slowly followed his clan.

"Come on, champ," Hank said to Kip. "Let's go home and clean you up. You look like a bum."

27

Hᴀɴᴋ ʜᴜʀʀɪᴇᴅ ɪɴᴛᴏ the house ahead of us, found Annabelle in the kitchen, and a few seconds later came back to wave us in through the front. I got Kip into the bathroom, where he washed up, then slipped him into his bedroom and clean clothes.

"She'll want to know how they got so mussed," he told me as he stared at the battle uniform.

"So we won't lie. The idea's not to have her see you looking like a used mop. How do you feel?"

"Tired."

"You got a right."

"Is that all I'm supposed to feel after a fight?"

"You can feel sore."

He touched the lump over his ear gingerly and gave me a small grin.

"I beat him, didn't I?"

"Sure thing. Scored a technical knockout. Old Toughy was tickled pink when I stopped it—don't you forget that."

He turned gloomy.

"Duke said there'd be another time."

"I don't think so. Toughy's not going to want any more."

Annabelle appeared in the door and studied her son. I guessed Hank had been telling her what happened. Her lips were tight.

For the first time since the Toughy thing began, Kip grinned all out.

"I beat him," he said. "He hurt his hand on my head and I split his lip and gave him a bloody nose."

She stared at him. The bruises from Toughy's attack a couple days back still showed, but the new fight left him with little more than scuffed cheeks and a lump over his left ear.

Annabelle frowned at me. "I guess you're pretty proud of yourself."

"No. He did it all on his own. Hardly paid any attention to my advice."

She gazed at her son sadly, shaking her head. "Okay, get ready for bed. You need a rest. I'm glad you didn't get hurt."

Kip's face turned long after she left.

"Why isn't she glad? Why's she sore at you?"

"Don't worry about it. Go brush your teeth and just be glad you've still got 'em all, okay?"

"I'll never understand women," he muttered, and went back to the bathroom.

The telephone rang as I headed toward the kitchen. When I got there Annabelle said it was Al Hamilton for me.

"I got your mouth organ," he said. "What's more, I got a girl willing to show Carrie how to play it."

"Another cousin?"

"Yeah, how'd you know?"

"It came to me in a dream. Will this cousin invite Carrie over and let me come around?"

"She will if you bring your nephew, Hank. She's his age and thinks he's keen, as they say."

He said the cousin's name was Lou. She'd call Carrie on Tuesday to see what could be worked out.

Annabelle was waiting for me when I hung up.

"I appreciate what you were trying to do," she said. "I even think it was fine for you to teach him how to defend himself from bullies. That was mature and reasonable. What I hate is that you arranged a fight. That was stupid. How do you think it would have been if he'd fought that little gorilla and lost? Heard that gang jeering him? I know the O'Keefes and what a terror that Toughy is to all his schoolmates. It's a miracle Kip won—you can't take credit. So if he'd lost and you went in and beat the whole gang to a bloody pulp, what good would it have done? Did you give one second's thought to what could've happened? Kip's not like you or Hank or Scott. You're fighting roosters, but he's not like that and never will be. He's a sensitive child—you can't make him into one of you."

She started to cry. I felt like a prize asshole and tried to calm her, but she jerked loose and ran to her room.

She was right, of course. What could I say?

$\triangledown$

28

ANNABELLE WAS ALL over being mad by Wednesday. She couldn't hold a grudge because she was certain the wrongs her family committed were all through foolishness or momentary thoughtlessness—perfectly normal human failings that didn't require forgiving.

No doubt she had a serious talk with Kip about how pointless fighting was, but she did it in private and he never mentioned it to me.

The arrangements with Al Hamilton's young cousin got complicated—it was Thursday before we could work it all out.

Meanwhile Stella had a conference with Annabelle, which ended with Hank being invited to go down to the clothing store and help out as a clerk. It worked fine. He was a natural clotheshorse, and his friends immediately started coming around to gab about murders and wound up buying clothes. I suspected Stella was cagey enough to figure that's what would happen.

A friend of Hank's lent me a bike and I went pedaling around town with Kip, figuring it'd provide him a bodyguard for a time. He asked me to tell stories of cowboying and scrapes I got into. The cowboying wasn't as interesting as the movies he'd seen, and most of the scrapes I could remember weren't ones Annabelle would approve of, so I got into things like experiences in France during the war to end wars. He liked the tale about me tearing down a French back road on a military motorcycle, hitting a stone fence, and flying into a canal one night. The motorbike had been a total loss, but all I got was wet. Hiking back to the post in soggy clothes on a cool night had been the most painful part of the experience.

When we got back home Annabelle greeted us with news that the trial had been scheduled to open next Monday. She said I had to do something right away. From the way folks were talking, it seemed clear to her no jury in Red Ford would find Stella innocent. I assured her I was still working on the case, and she tried not to look doubtful while she stared at me straddling the borrowed bike.

After supper I spotted Darlene sitting on her back step, brushing her freshly washed hair. She gave me her dreamy smile, tilting her head when I came close.

"You heard about the trial being scheduled?"

Her smile faded as she nodded her head and lowered the brush to her lap.

I asked if she was worried about testifying.

She nodded. "Actually, I worry most about Carrie. I've tried to convince the prosecuting attorney she's not competent to testify. She is, of course, but it will upset her so badly. She's terribly sensitive. If the defense goes after her, I just don't know . . ."

"I wondered about that. The last time you told me how shy she was, she showed up at the door in your house and talked to me with no trouble at all. I think you're over-defensive."

"She fools you. I'll admit, at times, she even fools me. But I do know her better than anyone else; and that time with you was a world apart from what happens in a courtroom. Will you be coming over tonight?"

She watched the place where she'd get the signal and I quickly sat down to hide it.

"Probably not," I said, trying for casual I didn't feel. "Annabelle's all tore up about the whole business, and she'd near die if she thought I was fooling around with a witness who might get her pal convicted."

"Does she suspect—?"

"I'm afraid so," I lied.

She lifted the brush and stroked her hair slowly. "I guess you think a lot of your sister."

"She's as fine as they come."

"I know she's terribly loyal and a wonderful mother. But be honest, she is awfully naive, don't you think?"

"Maybe. But she's not stupid."

"Oh, I wasn't suggesting that. It's just that terribly loyal people can sometimes be taken advantage of by their friends. Do you think you'll be staying in town after the trial is over?"

"It depends on how things go."

"I hope you will stay, whatever happens. Does it bother you that I'm pushing?"

"Bother's not quite it. If things go right, yeah, I'd like to see more of you."

"You haven't really seen all of me yet. I think about us a lot and keep thinking of more we could do. You're very wonderful, you know. Such energy and eagerness—a wonderful, youthful quality in a man with so much experience."

"I seem to remember you saying something about where flattery'd get me."

"I did, and I hope it works for me, if you know what I mean."

I did, and wanted to take her inside right then but held off, thinking it'd be a crummy thing to do right when I was working to finagle her daughter into a deal the next day to find out what really happened. If Carrie had murdered Aaron and I got her to admit it, I'd feel like a total asshole if I had balled her mother the night before. Obviously Darlene was using sex to sidetrack me, but that seemed okay. Women have damned few ways to outfight men; I figure they got a right to use any they can find. I sure as hell didn't worry about her making a fool of me.

When I stood up she gave me a smile full of promise and trust. It made me feel like a slob, especially when it also made me suspicious.

You come right down to it, I didn't really give a damn who did in Aaron or Fox. It'd have been lots better to leave things alone, except that might cause Stella to take the rap, and I couldn't let that happen even if she was too slow in bed.

I wished to hell things could be simple.

29

H<small>ANK'S NEW JOB</small> at the clothing store made him unavailable for the meeting at Al Hamilton's cousin's place until after supper. It took some talking to get him at all, because he remembered the cousin as an overweight kid who gazed at him so worshipfully in freshman history class that all his buddies made a joke of it.

We were met at the front door by Mrs. Elkins, cousin Lou's mother, who was tall, slim, and dark as a gypsy. She barely glanced at me, but smiled at Hank, showing teeth bright as a lightbulb, then directed us into the parlor left of the entrance. It was a small room crowded with maroon furniture, antimacassars, doilies, phony flowers, and throw rugs.

Cousin Lou was a pleasant surprise. From Hank's story I'd expected a tub, but this kid was padded only in the right places. Her dark hair was glossy, and she wore just enough makeup to give a man ideas without making him feel the paint would run when he started smooching. Her brown eyes hit Hank first; her smile was enough to make him dizzy. She gave me a glance that was pure politeness, and I'd have bet she'd not recognize me if we met the next day. Hank was all she saw or wanted to see.

Carrie seemed pale and fragile in contrast, and shrank into the wingbacked chair she was parked in when we arrived. I moved over to her, spotted the harmonica in her hands, and asked if she'd already begun learning how to play it.

She immediately began to bloom, turning from shy to

eager. I sat on the couch that almost touched her chair and
asked if she had managed to find the lost harmonica yet.

She shook her head and the smile faded.

"You don't know how it got lost, huh?"

"Mama says it's because I was careless."

Mrs. Elkins, after a few words with Hank, left us, heading
for the kitchen. Hank settled on an easy chair at the far end
of the couch Carrie was on, and Lou took the middle space.

I heard him say she had changed a lot since they were
freshmen. She smiled and said she was glad he noticed. They
kept smiling at each other.

"What've you learned on that?" I asked Carrie, pointing
at the harmonica in her lap.

"Scales."

"Want to show me?"

At first she said no, but her smile came back. I could tell
she wanted to and a little coaxing brought her to it. She blew
the notes with deep concentration, exact as a machine,
smiling triumphantly after going up and down the scale.
Cousin Lou smiled at her; so did Hank. She blushed
furiously and ducked her head.

"That's great. You just learned that today?"

"Uh-huh. I can do it faster."

"Go ahead."

There was a slight slur between do and re, so she went
back and did it over and got it right.

"You're going to be a natural."

"Mama says Aaron was a natural musician."

"You heard him play his horn?"

"Uh-huh. I could hear him in his house in the summer
when their windows were open. Sometimes he brought his
saxophone over to our house and played for us."

"Your mother like that?"

"Oh, yeah. She loved it."

"You think your mother liked Aaron pretty well?"

She gave me a glance of innocent wonder. "Of course."

"I guess you were pretty good friends."

She nodded, sadly.

Hank said something that made Lou laugh, then she got up and went over to a piano in the corner. Hank followed. Lou played a few notes and started a number I couldn't name.

I leaned closer to Carrie.

"What happened the night Aaron died?"

She looked at the mouth organ, turning it in her hands. Then she met my eyes.

"There was an awful noise outside my room."

"Did you look out?"

She shook her head. "We were afraid."

"Your mother was with you?"

"Uh-huh."

"Did you hear him come into the house?"

"No."

"But you knew he was coming, didn't you?"

She looked over toward the piano, where Hank was smiling down at Lou while she played and gazed back at him.

"I'm not to tell that," said Carrie.

"Why?"

" 'Cause people'd think I was bad if they knew."

"Darlene told you that, huh?"

She stared into her lap again. The slim hands fondled the mouth organ gently.

"Where was your mother when you heard the noise?"

"With me. In my room. We were both sitting on the bed."

"What happened when the noise stopped?"

"Mama hugged me and we listened. Somebody went down the stairs and out, I guess."

"Was your door locked?"

"Yes," she whispered.

"Darlene locked it, huh?"

She nodded.

"Had you told your mother that Aaron said he'd come to see you when you were alone?"

"He told me not to tell her."

"And you thought you were bad not to?"

She nodded slowly. "He said if I didn't let him come he'd die. But then he died anyway, didn't he?"

"Had he come to see you when you were alone before?"

She took a deep breath and let it out before nodding.

"What'd he do when you were alone together?"

"Cuddled me."

"Hugs? Maybe kisses?"

"Uh-huh."

"He touch you lots of places?"

"All over my face. Kisses. And he touched my hair and talked to me real sweet."

"He didn't touch you anyplace else?"

"He hugged me real close."

"You touch him?"

"When he put his hands on my face, I touched them. That's all right. Mama told me there was nothing wrong with that."

"How'd that come up?"

She didn't understand the question, so I explained and she said it had come up on the afternoon before Aaron died. She had asked her mother what a girl should do when a man was awfully nice to her. Darlene had said to be careful and explained in detail where she should not allow herself to be touched or persuaded to touch a man. She had allowed that touching his hands when he fondled her face wasn't really bad, but it might not be wise because then he might want her to do other things.

"Did she ask you how come you wanted to know all this?" I asked.

"Uh-huh. I told her I thought I should know in case anybody was special nice to me, and she said it was good to think ahead."

"Did she ask if you had anybody in mind?"

"No."

Obviously she hadn't found it necessary to ask. Aaron was the only one who'd been around often and close enough.

I asked more questions and became convinced he hadn't made any attempt to go all the way or even tried to arouse anything but affection. I worked her back to the night of the killing. She insisted she had been with her mother the entire evening, right up until Darlene unlocked their door and went out to find Aaron murdered on the stairway landing. Darlene told Carrie that Stella had done it because she was jealous of Carrie. Carrie must say nothing to anyone about it all, because if people even guessed that she had let Aaron into her room at any time, they would think it was her fault the murder happened—that she'd been doing things with Aaron that were awful and a sin. She did not explain what the awful things might have been, and Carrie was afraid to ask.

30

L OU WAS WILLING to let me walk Carrie home, but her mother caught up with us at the door and nixed the notion.

"Darlene'd never forgive me if I let a man alone with her baby. She's really beautiful, isn't she?"

Carrie blushed, ducked her head, and smiled happily.

Hank stayed back with Lou. I let Mrs. Elkins get on ahead about half a block. After Carrie was safe inside and Mrs. Elkins had gone home, I waited awhile before drifting across the back lot and tapping on Darlene's rear door.

Several seconds passed before she came and stood behind the screen in silence.

I said hi.

"Carrie says you were at the Elkins house."

Her voice was cold as an outhouse in January.

"Uh-huh. Went over to keep Hank company."

"And you asked her questions about Aaron."

"That's right."

"So what more do you want from me?"

"All I can get."

"I think you've already had it."

Her face was a pale blur in the dim light—I couldn't read her expression. Finally I asked, "Had you been over at Gene Fox's that night?"

"You're really something," she said in a voice of sad wonder. "I thought you really liked me. When you made love to me it was like you thought I was something wonderful. And then you sneak around, talk to Carrie, and try to make her say her mother's a murderer. How could you do that?"

"I didn't try to make her say anything. I asked to find out stuff I had to know."

"Was that it? Or were you just playing me along from the start, thinking you'd do your precious sister a favor and find somebody besides her friend to pay for Aaron's murder? Did you really think I'd let you make love to me so soon after I'd killed a man?"

"Darlene, I haven't known you a week, but every time I tried to ask you questions we wound up in a clinch. You're sexier than hell and I'd love to go to bed with you right now, but I've got to know for sure what happened that night. You ought to understand that."

After a few seconds of silence she pushed the screen open and told me to come in.

I was ready for a kiss or the knife, but she turned her back and walked through the kitchen into the parlor. I trailed along, barely able to see her form ahead of me. She sat on the couch; I settled beside her.

"I didn't go over to Gene's that night," she said. "I was waiting for Aaron here."

"What were you going to do?"

"Give him a piece of my mind."

"Through a locked door?"

"I was going to let him try to open it—then I'd have unlocked it and faced him down. I was very angry that he'd taken advantage of Carrie and me."

"Why'd Aaron think you wouldn't be home?"

She lowered her head a moment, lifted it, and sighed.

"You're going to think I'm awful."

"I doubt it."

"You've got to understand how it's been for me. You know I'm a loving woman, and I've been a widow for ever so long. It's very lonely—"

"Sure, I can see that."

"Most men are leery of a woman with a daughter like Carrie. The ones I've met who weren't turned out more interested in her than me, you know what I'm saying?"

I wanted to tell her I'd think she was perfectly normal to start messing with Gene Fox, but figured it would be better to let her spell it out her own way. Finally she did.

"A few months back I started going over to Gene's house after Carrie went to sleep on weekends. I told you, she sleeps hard and I felt she was perfectly safe. I never stayed long. It was nothing like with you, nothing at all. He was, well, he didn't understand about women—or even care. Aaron must've seen me going across the alley and figured it out a while back. He came over to see Carrie lots of days, as you know, and I left them in the house alone a couple times when I was working in the garden. That's when he must've started making up to her. And when he asked her to wait up for him, she didn't know quite what to make of it and couldn't help asking me questions that made me realize what he was up to."

"Okay. Did you tell Gene why you wouldn't be coming over that Saturday night?"

She nodded.

"Was it your idea he use Stella's knife to make it look like a jealous wife did the job?"

She drew back.

"How could you think such a thing?"

"I just don't see Gene as a guy with any imagination. He was sore as a boil over Aaron collecting half the income from the store without lifting a hand to make it go. I figure he hated him for being so nuts about his dumb little band, as though being a store manager were something beneath him. He wanted the store to himself, and when he heard Aaron knew he was being screwed and there'd be trouble about it, he had to do something."

"Why'd he want Stella to take the blame? She was his mistress, too, you know. Gene wanted everything Aaron had—his store, his wife, everything. She was more of what Aaron didn't have the sense to appreciate."

"So this is all stuff you told the police."

"I didn't tell them Carrie agreed to let Aaron in. They wouldn't have believed she was innocent. They'd think she was a little slut, and all these dirty-minded pigs in town, they'd love to have believed the worst."

"How'd you know Aaron was wise to Gene cheating him at the store?"

There was a second's pause before she answered.

"Carrie knew. Aaron told her. He told her everything."

"And Carrie tells you everything."

"Yes. She can't lie, and she's no good at trying to hold back if you question her—as you learned."

"Okay. So you told Gene that Aaron was wise to him, didn't you?"

"What makes you think that?"

"I think you'd do anything to protect Carrie, Darlene. That's not hard to understand. Not at all."

"You think I arranged the murder, don't you?"

"You sure as hell made it possible."

"I wish I hadn't," she said, slumping low on the couch.

"How'd you arrange for Stella to kill Gene?"

"Oh, Carl, I didn't do any such thing. I'm not like that. I didn't really plan any of it, it all just worked itself out."

"Yeah, but you gave it a nice nudge where it was needed."

"It was all Gene's fault. He was crazy. He tried to make me promise to say I'd been sleeping with him the night he killed Aaron so he'd have an alibi. He said if I didn't and they tried to prove he was the murderer, he'd tell them why Aaron was in my house, that Aaron had been making love to Carrie. If he couldn't convince them I'd killed Aaron, he'd at least make everybody think Carrie was a slut and I was a whore. So I explained to him very carefully what stories like that would do to his precious business. Pretty soon it wasn't hard to convince him he'd be better off if he and Stella gave each other alibis."

"That must have been pretty tricky when he did the murder so it looked like Stella was the killer."

"Well, that wasn't my idea."

"Did you admit to the police you were sleeping with Gene?"

"I never slept with him. And of course I didn't tell them the rest."

"You know if he told them he'd had you?"

"I'm sure he didn't. After all, he wasn't a complete fool, you know."

"No? So how come it didn't dawn on him that having everybody know he'd been screwing Aaron's wife would be as tough on business as them knowing he'd been diddling you?"

"It probably did. He was a great one for figuring the angles. So he cut his own throat. If you can prove that, then your sister can be happy seeing Stella set free."

I was silent. Slowly, she moved closer.

"Don't worry. It can all work out. I won't say anything to hurt Stella, honest. Everybody'll think Gene killed Aaron, then later, when he realized it was going to catch up with him, he committed suicide."

"And you didn't maybe make him see it all that way?"

She shrugged. "I just told him the facts. I didn't tell him what to do about it."

She moved until her hip was against mine.

"Did Gene ever show interest in Carrie?" I asked.

She moved away and stood up. "No. I think I heard something upstairs. I better check on Carrie. Will you wait?"

"No. I've got to go."

"He killed himself, you know. That wasn't my doing."

"Or Stella's."

"That's right. So everything has worked out as well as it can for everybody."

She moved toward the stairs, and I let myself out as she climbed to Carrie.

31

"W HERE ARE THE boys?" I asked Annabelle when I found her reading in the living room.

She set her *Redbook* aside and said they'd gone to a movie downtown.

I sat down and stared at her for a few moments. She actually managed to stare back and look innocent.

"How come," I began, "you never told me Stella was getting laid by Gene Fox?"

She reddened and folded her hands in her lap.

"What a crude way to put it. I didn't tell you because I knew you'd take it just this way and you'd get the wrong idea."

"Ah. Well, sister, how about you tell me now what the right idea is?"

"It's very simple. Stella's been a neglected and unhappy woman for years. Gene came along, a handsome, intelligent man with no family in the world. He cared passionately about the store. It all began with her trying to encourage his success as a manager and, well, things just sort of went on from there. It was a very natural thing to come about. They couldn't help themselves."

"You mean it was okay as long as they weren't just crazy about each other's bodies?"

"Don't try to make fun of me, Carl, it doesn't become you. If you stop to think at all, you know how bad I must feel about all of this. I admit, Stella was very foolish and impulsive, but that's all it was. I mean, for heaven's sake, her husband didn't care a thing about her. They hadn't slept together in years. She's a lovely woman who needs to be loved like everyone else."

"She ever make a play for Scott?"

She managed to look shocked.

"Certainly not! What in the world would give you that ridiculous notion?"

"Just wondered. You know that Fox was being kind to your neighbor, Darlene?"

The shocked expression became even greater.

"Come now, where'd you get that notion?"

"She just admitted it to me, half an hour ago."

She shook her head. "You got that out of her? Good lord, Carl, you certainly do have a way with widows, don't you?"

"I never had much luck getting facts from Stella."

Her shocked expression abruptly turned wise. "You got something else, though, didn't you?"

"Don't get cute. The next time you want my help for one of your friends, just level with me all the way, okay?"

"What're you saying?"

"I'm leaving tomorrow. Stella's getting out of this. The cops haven't admitted it yet, but they found Fox's prints on the knife by the bed, so it'll get tagged as a suicide. I don't think anybody really wants it to be anything else—suicide's the easy answer and they'll settle for that."

Annabelle's eyes narrowed. "You still suspect Stella, don't you? Because she lied to you."

"Everybody lies to me. Even my little sister. Don't worry about it, you're getting what you wanted."

"Why're you mad at me?"

"I'm not mad at you. Just a little sore because you held out and made a sucker of me for a while."

"You don't believe Gene killed himself, do you?"

"I don't know."

"You suspect Stella made it look that way."

"Did she?"

"Do you think I'd keep that from you if I knew?"

"I hope not."

"You know I wouldn't. That's not a thing I'd hide from you and you must know it."

I nodded. She wouldn't ever try to dig that deep, even if she were capable of probing for hidden evils in her closest friends.

She sat up and leaned toward me.

"The trouble is, you think Darlene did it but you can't prove that and don't really want to, do you? So it's eating you. And you've decided to let her get away with it because you sympathize with her desperation to protect Carrie. That's how you rationalize it all, isn't it? That it was a particularly motherish thing of self-defense. She arranged to have Gene kill Aaron to protect Carrie, then she killed Gene for the same reason. Maybe he was a threat to Carrie, too . . . or just as bad. He might have blamed her for the murder to make things easier on himself. If Darlene went to jail, who'd take care of Carrie? You'd have felt responsible like you always do."

She sat back and smiled tenderly.

"What a cream puff you are, Carl. All the tough-guy front is a phony. No wonder women love you."

What the hell. Annabelle always was a screwball, so I said sure, and let it go at that.

The case against Stella was put away after the investigators agreed the fingerprints on the knife were unquestionably Fox's. That was fortified by an auditor's report on the store's finances, which disclosed that Fox had been taking over three-quarters of the profits from the store's business—instead of the authorized half—and was in imminent peril of being exposed and losing everything.

The verdict on the case was murder and suicide by Gene Fox.

Hank drove back to the Wilcox Hotel in Corden on Friday, and I drove east into Minnesota, figuring to find sign painting jobs through the rest of the summer.

Annabelle wrote in late August that Darlene had put her

house up for sale and was planning a move to California with Carrie.

In September I got word that Stella was dining once a week with her lawyer. Annabelle didn't offer any criticism, but I got the weird impression that she was telling me this as a confession that perhaps her judgment about her friends could, on rare occasions, be flawed.